The Mercury Cup

T. R. BURCH

The Mercury Cup

A DRAGON BOOK

GRANADA

London Toronto Sydney New York

Published in paperback by Granada Publishing Limited in 1983

ISBN 0 583 30570 9

First published in Great Britain by
Granada Publishing 1982
Copyright © T. R. Burch 1982

Granada Publishing Limited
Frogmore, St Albans, Herts AL2 2NF
and
36 Golden Square, London W1R 4AH
515 Madison Avenue, New York, NY 10022, USA
117 York Street, Sydney, NSW 2000, Australia
60 International Blvd, Rexdale, Ontario, R9W 6J2, Canada
61 Beach Road, Auckland, New Zealand

Printed and bound in Great Britain by
Cox and Wyman Ltd, Reading

Set in Plantin

Granada ®
Granada Publishing ®

For Carolyn,
with many thanks

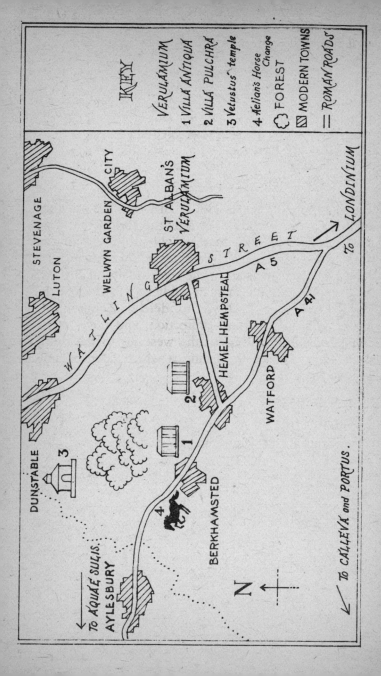

KEY

VERULAMIUM
1 VILLA ANTIQUA
2 VILLA PULCHRA
3 Vetustus' temple
4 Aelian's Horse
  Change
🌳 FOREST
▨ MODERN TOWNS
= ROMAN ROADS

STEVENAGE
LUTON
DUNSTABLE
WELWYN GARDEN CITY
ST ALBAN'S
VERULAMIUM

WATLING STREET

HEMEL HEMPSTEAD
A5
A41
WATFORD

BERKHAMSTED

TO AQUAE SULIS.
AYLESBURY

3

2

1

4

N

TO CALLEVA and PORTUS.

TO LONDINIUM

Historical Note

For the first four centuries A.D. Britain was a province of the Roman Empire. Towards the end of that time the country had been increasingly subject to attacks from gangs of Saxons and Angles who came over the North Sea and penetrated the river valleys of Britain. By A.D. 410 all the Roman soldiers had been withdrawn from the province to defend Rome itself. Britain was left without protection, and many of its inhabitants fled, either to the west, or to the south across the channel to Armorica which later became known as Brittany.

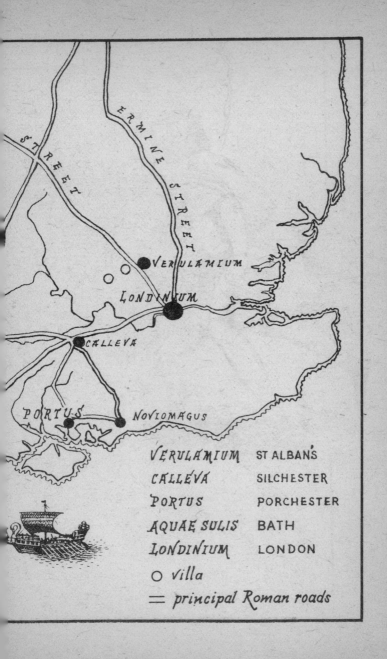

STREET

ERMINE STREET

●VERULAMIUM

○ ○

LONDINIUM ●

●CALLEVA

PORTUS ● ● NOVIOMAGUS

VERULAMIUM	ST ALBAN'S
CALLEVA	SILCHESTER
PORTUS	PORCHESTER
AQUAE SULIS	BATH
LONDINIUM	LONDON
○ villa	
= principal Roman roads	

Chapter One

Aquilo was collecting blackberries on the hillside above the Villa Antiqua. Every so often he looked across the bracken towards the fields which surrounded the villa, and he could see little men like ants scurrying about on errands. The big covered carriage was in the yard. Nobody had used it for years, but now, on the hottest day of the year, out it trundled. Aquilo could imagine the squeaking of the iron-bound wheels, and the axles which had not been greased for months.

He had an earthenware bowl for those blackberries he did not eat at once. Why was he collecting them, anyway? 'Go and gather blackberries' his father had said. Aquilo had looked surprised, but he did what he was told, because his father was clearly in a worry about something. A strange little messenger had come to the villa last night – perhaps he had something to do with it.

There weren't many people on the roads recently. Old Vetustus at the temple had told him that once the roads were full of merchants and soldiers and officials and couriers – but that was in the good old days before governors of Britain had become too big for their boots and began to think of themselves as Emperors. They had taken the soldiers to fight for them on the continent or even further to Rome itself, and few of the soldiers ever came back to tell what had happened to the rest.

The roads weren't safe any more – that's what they said. At any time you might meet a band of fugitive slaves, or, even worse, a war party of Saxons. Aquilo had never met any in all of his thirteen years of life, but the stories of old Vetustus lost nothing in the telling.

If you followed the stream, people said, you would arrive eventually at London. Aquilo had never been that far. Once he had gone to Verulamium and wondered at the great stone walls surrounding the city, and wondered even more that anyone should want to live in those cramped streets.

He sat on a hillock and watched the activity in the yard. Odd that there was nobody in the fields now. Most of the harvesting had been done already: it had been early this year, and the grain was dry and would not need the roasting it usually got to preserve it. But there were still a good many jobs that the slaves should have been doing.

Aquilo looked down at the bowl and found it empty. He was not surprised. The blackberries were good this year, like everything else.

Aquilo stirred uneasily on the hillock of grass. He liked to know what was going on round him, and obviously on this occasion he didn't. Well, now that he'd eaten all the blackberries, he might as well go and find out.

He got up, brushing away the flies which had been using his legs as a dancing-floor. Some of the black-berries, he noticed, had got squashed on his tunic, but it was an old one, anyway, and he didn't suppose anyone would notice an extra bit of pattern. They were all too busy.

He pushed a hand over his head. People liked to

make fun of his almost white hair. For himself, he was rather proud of it, if he thought about it at all: at least it was different from everybody else's dark hair. His mother said it went with his dark blue eyes – but a lot of the things his mother said embarrassed him. She couldn't realise that he had grown up, or nearly so.

That was another cause of annoyance. Why didn't they *tell* him things? Things he ought to know, like how to run the farm, and keep the slaves contented but controlled, and look after the horses and other animals. Felix would always tell him if he asked – if Felix was in a better temper than usual. Felix was his father's steward at the Villa Antiqua, a little man with a thatch of thick black hair, middle-aged, surly, and morose. Just occasionally, when he opened a jar of wine, he would unbend and talk. Aquilo had always been fascinated by his stories. His parents told him not to spend so much of his time with the slaves, but at least they were company.

So was Brutus. A big brown bushy-tailed dog, which was supposed to have been trained for hunting – that's what they said when his father bought him at Verulamium. But they had soon found him out: he was lazy, fat, soft, and greedy.

'Brutus!' Aquilo called, and the long grass by the thicket of birch trees moved slightly.

'Here, boy! I know you're there. You'll regret it if I have to come and fetch you.'

Muttering to himself, Aquilo beat his way through the brambles and ferns to the thicket. He had a stick in his hand, but that was for the nettles, not Brutus. One moist brown eye observed his progress. The bushy tail swept the grass, scattering a little cloud of dust.

'Brutus! Food!' That brought him. He crawled out

of the undergrowth and stood before Aquilo with his tongue hanging out. Little drops of moisture rolled off his jaws and tickled Aquilo's feet. Aquilo laughed.

'Oh, all right' he said, bringing out a small dark cake from the leather pouch at his belt. He had been saving it for himself, but Brutus' need was just as great. He broke the cake into two pieces. 'Here you are, pig.' The dog gobbled the dry crumbs and nosed Aquilo's knees for more. Aquilo hastily put the rope which he had been holding behind his back round the dog's neck, and fastened it with a running knot. Boy and dog set off down the hill towards the villa.

It was about midday when they arrived. The yard in front of the long low villa was empty now, except for the carriage which was piled with boxes and sacks and bundles. A man lay sprawled at the foot of the steps leading to the corridor along the front of the building. His eyes were closed.

Aquilo walked past him and climbed the steps. He found his father in the chair reserved for him in the farm-office.

There was a small bronze box on his knees.

'Hullo,' said Aquilo. 'Want any help?'

His father snapped the box shut and turned the key.

'You startled me, Aquilo,' he grumbled. He was tugging at a leather bag into which he was trying to push the box.

'That's your money box,' Aquilo remarked. There was a figure of the god Mercury engraved on the top of the box. 'What are you going to do with it?'

'Shush!' His father sounded irritable. 'Just get it in this confounded leather, will you? That's it. Now, forget the whole thing.'

'Why?'

'Because I say so.'

Aquilo watched his father tapping his fingers on the arms of the chair.

'What's the carriage for?' he asked at length.

'H'm? Travelling, of course. Now, off you go. I haven't time.'

Aquilo wandered off to find someone else. He could hear his mother in her room, but she seemed to be having a row with a slave, so Aquilo thought it wiser not to interrupt. He went outside and sat on the steps. Brutus lay at his feet, gasping in the heat. Aquilo looked at the sleeping figure of the man with his head on the first step. He put one foot on the man's chest and pushed. One bleary eye winked at him.

'You've no need to do that,' the man said. 'If you want something, you just ask, and I'll consider it.'

Aquilo grinned. He liked the Brock. 'Wake up!' he said.

'I am awake.' The Brock settled his hands over his stomach. His hair flopped down over his face, black hair, with one streak of white, so that the face gave one an impression of a badger. He had always been called the Brock.

'Come on, Brock! Tell me what's happening. The carriage. And father counting his money. What's it all for?'

The Brock chuckled fatly. 'We're all off on our travels.'

'London?'

'No point in going that way when you're running away.'

'Who's running?'

'Caius Vincentius Clemens, your honoured and respected father, young sir.'

15

'He's not! Who from, anyway?'

The Brock shifted his weight on the steps, but his eyes were still closed. 'Me, I like living. And I don't like what I've heard of Saxons.'

'Saxons? Here?'

'That's what the gossip says. That's why everybody's running. Except me.'

'Where *is* everybody?'

'Packing up. Like I said. All ready to run. You will too, I expect.'

Aquilo stared at Brutus' shaggy head. Some burrs were sticking to the dogs ears, and he began to work them loose.

'But we can't take everything!' His eyes glanced round the wide yard and the long ranges of buildings. 'What about all this?'

'You only take what you need on a journey, the rest you leave. It's easier.'

'So we're leaving everything here, is that it?'

The Brock whistled through his teeth. 'I keep my eyes open,' he said. 'People think I don't know what goes on, but I do. You ask your father what he was doing last night. About midnight, I should say. Up by the temple. Go on, you ask him.'

Aquilo got up with sudden decision. 'I will' he said. 'Somebody might tell me where we're all going.'

He ran up the steps. His father was no longer in the office. The house was unnaturally quiet. The only person he saw as he came out of the office was Felix, the steward. For once he looked almost pleased.

'Have you seen my father?' Aquilo demanded.

'Out in the granary,' Felix replied. 'If you want to take anything, you'd better get it now. We'll be off before dark.'

'Yes, but – '

'The draughts board. I thought you might like to take that.'

Aquilo turned and ran along the corridor: he had no time just at the moment to think about draughts boards.

The Brock still lay sprawled at the bottom of the steps and Brutus was not far away. Aquilo snorted to himself as he passed them. Alike as two peas they were, lazy and self-satisfied. Even when everybody else was up and about, doing things.

He didn't know what made him turn back to the Brock. There was something strange about him,

17

something that hadn't been there before. Aquilo's eyes widened. He took a step nearer.

The Brock's hair still flopped over his brown face, his hands were still clasped over his fat stomach. But the handle of a knife was sticking out of his chest, glistening in the sun, and he was dead.

Chapter Two

Caius Vincentius Clemens, owner of the Villa Antiqua and a number of other farms within a mile or two, was more annoyed than troubled by the death of one of his slaves. It had happened at an inconvenient time; it interrupted the preparations for departure.

When Aquilo ran into the granary to tell him, his father had not at first wanted to listen. He was addressing all the estate workers, giving them their final orders, seeing that everything was arranged.

Aquilo stood at his side, trying to attract his attention. He knew better than to interrupt his father when in full flow: it would be like trying to stop the mill-race when the gates were opened and the thrust of imprisoned water turned the great wheel.

Vincentius turned an irritated and bothered face towards him. He was a fussy old man, with hardly any hair, and yellowed skin, but he was still the master.

'What is it, boy? Can't you see I am busy?'

'It's the Brock. Out in the yard. He's dead.'

'Not from overwork, I'll be bound,' his father snorted. 'Felix, take a couple of fellows and see to it.'

'Sir.'

A stir of interest passed along the rows of faces. Heavy feet kicked the dust which hung like a mist in the sunbeams.

'But somebody's *killed* him,' Aquilo insisted. 'There was a knife.'

'Knife? Where?'

'Sticking out of his chest. Come and see.'

'I shall do nothing of the sort. Far too busy. Felix will see to it. Now, where was I?'

The voice droned on, as dry as the scattered husks on the floor. Aquilo slipped away. It was cleaner out in the sunshine.

Felix was standing on the steps at the front of the house. Two large men stood a few paces away, awaiting orders. Their hair was matted, and their skin was like leather. Their arms hung loosely at their sides.

'What are you going to do with him, Felix?' Aquilo demanded.

Felix jerked a thumb at the stream which flowed by the side of the villa.

'You can't do that!' Aquilo protested hotly.

Felix gave him a long cool look. 'Times change,' he said at length. 'Perhaps you're right. Boys, take him to the copse of alder.'

The two big men grunted, lifted the Brock, carried him like a baby over their shoulders, and marched off in step. The Brock's head swung in time to the rhythm.

Aquilo turned away. He felt sick.

'Will they do all the right things, Felix?'

'As much as they remember. It will be enough. The Brock will forgive them.'

'But who did it to him, Felix? Who knifed him?'

The little man's shoulders moved. 'Who knows? Did you not see?'

'Me? He was alive when I left him to look for my father. I can't have been away for more than a moment or two. Then, when I came back . . . *Why*, Felix? Why would anyone want to do that to the Brock? He never harmed anybody in his life. Doesn't anybody *care*?'

'The living need more care than the dead.'

'What's that supposed to mean?' Aquilo dropped to the steps, his eyes searching the place where the Brock had lain in the sun. 'I'll find him,' he said softly, 'whoever it was who did it. *Somebody* has to care.'

A hubbub of voices from the buildings beyond the villa broke the hot stillness. Vincentius came puffing round the corner, making for the steps.

'Ah, Felix! You have seen to the necessary arrangements? Good. We shall be off within the hour.'

'Sir.' Felix shuffled away towards the slaves' quarters. Aquilo could hear his gruff voice commanding, reproving, organising. Felix always got things done.

'Now, then. All ready for departure, are we?' Vincentius seemed to notice Aquilo for the first time. 'Don't just sit around catching flies, boy. We must be up and doing.'

'What for, father?' Aquilo looked up at his father without moving.

'Has nobody told you? Really, Aquilo, I sometimes wonder whether you or that useless dog of yours is the more stupid.'

'Nobody's told me anything.'

'No, I don't suppose they have.' Vincentius sighed. He pulled his long tunic together, and sat down on the steps by Aquilo's side. 'You see, Aquilo, it's like this. A peaceful valley, isn't it?'

Aquilo looked up in surprise. His blue eyes took in the sweep of the hills which enclosed the farm, the big wheel turned by the stream, the water-meadows, the yellow dusty fields stretching up the slopes till they met the ring of trees which divided the land from the hot bowl of the sky.

'I suppose it is,' he said. 'I never thought.'

'We've lived a very settled life here, seeing hardly a

21

soul for years past. Of course, it was all different when I was young. But recently, well, everything has been closing in, tightening round us like the rope on one of the big catapults.'

'Saxons?'

'Yes.' Vincentius was silent for a moment, watching a colony of ants busily occupied at the base of the steps. 'We're like those little creatures, Aquilo, just like that. Secure in our own small world, and not knowing that enemies may be lurking only a step away.' He brought one sandalled foot down heavily on the scurrying ants. 'Then the blow falls. News came last night. You remember Marcus at the Villa Pulchra?'

'Of course.'

Vincentius again fell silent. 'We should have known,' he said eventually, almost to himself.

'What about Marcus at the Villa Pulchra?' Aquilo prompted.

'A whole army of Saxons appeared there yesterday. Marcus' men put up a fight, of course, but they were outnumbered. Hopeless.'

'What happened?'

'The messenger who came last night said he was the only one to escape. The house is gone. These Saxons are all the same. They will have a riotous time at the Villa Pulchra, or what's left of it, till the food runs out, then they will be on the march to find somewhere else. They follow the streams as a rule. It won't be many days before they find this place. That's why we are going. Now do you understand?'

Aquilo tried to concentrate his mind on what his father was telling him, but all he could think of was the peaceful expression on the Brock's face as he lay at the foot of the steps with a dagger in his heart. A Saxon dagger?

He shivered, though the sun was still hot on his face.

'Where are we going, father?'

'By a route I've worked out, by way of Calleva to the coast. I have business friends at Portus, and we should be able to get a boat.'

Aquilo's head jerked up. 'Boat?'

'To Armorica. This province is finished, Aquilo. The Saxons can have it. In Armorica we can start another life. A safer life, I hope.'

Armorica. Across the sea. Aquilo knew enough to draw a map of it in his mind. The north-west corner of Gaul. Safety.

His father pulled himself to his feet. 'Come along, Aquilo, I have something to show you.'

Aquilo followed him to the study. It was cool and dark in the house, after the heat outside. Suddenly his father was all jollity, a strange and insincere good humour.

'We mustn't fall by the way, must we? We must all learn to rough it on the journey.'

'Yes, father.'

Vincentius produced a leather bag with a string to close its mouth at the top.

'There, that's yours. Well, open it, and have a look.'

Wonderingly, Aquilo did as he was told. Objects tumbled out onto the table. A bowl, a knife, a small set of tweezers and scissors, a leather water-bottle, and a pewter cup with two handles.

'There, what do you think? You have to look after it, you know, as though your survival depends on it.'

Suddenly Aquilo realised the truth. Behind this

23

cover of hearty laughter, his father was deeply worried. Afraid. His father was *afraid*.

He began to pack the things back in the leather bag. 'A nice cup, isn't it? Notice the design?'

Aquilo looked at the cup, felt the pattern engraved in the pewter. The god Mercury, with his winged hat, and his staff, and his winged sandals. His father's business sign.

'Yes, it's one of the old ones,' Vincentius said. 'Good solid pewter.'

'It wants cleaning.' Aquilo tried to sound helpful. 'It looks as though it's been in the fire. All black and sooty.'

Vincentius' forced laughter ceased. 'Nonsense, boy. It's better that way. People won't be able to see what it is. Put it away.'

Aquilo did as he was told.

Vincentius hurried out. Aquilo could hear him shouting in the yard. He looked round the cool room. It was, perhaps, the last time he would see it.

He heard his name called, and he ran out to the long corridor and down the steps. The procession of slaves, carriage, and baggage carts had formed in a long line, and the horses were already harnessed. Brutus was watching all this activity from a shady corner. Aquilo ran over to him and pulled the dog to his feet.

'Aquilo!' Vincentius called. 'Hurry up!'

Felix was busy shepherding the slaves at the back of the column. He saw Aquilo and told him to hurry.

'We're going,' he said. His usual moroseness was less noticeable, now that he had something to do. 'Got everything? What about that draughts board? And the dice?'

Aquilo took one look at the horses straining at the

24

front of the carriage, and raced off, calling out 'Shan't be long!' He *wanted* those games.

Vincentius stuck his head out of the carriage and shouted, but the vehicle was already moving, the iron tyres grinding on the cobbles, the driver cursing at the horses.

Still, he had plenty of time. He could easily run inside, get the board and the dice, and catch them up. He told Brutus to stay at the bottom of the steps, and raced along the corridor to the room at the end. He struggled with the big wooden lever which fastened the door, and tumbled in.

There it was! Under the bench. He grabbed the board, stuffed the dice into the pouch which hung at his belt, and turned to the door.

As he looked, the door swung in the wind and slammed shut. He heard the solid thud of the lever as it fell into its groove. He banged his fist against the wood, but he knew that it was useless. He couldn't get out.

Chapter Three

The sounds of the carriage and the marching slaves gradually faded away until only the sigh of the wind through the cracks in the door remained. It was dark, and becoming darker. In an hour or two night would be as black as the stoke-hole beneath the granary floor. He tried to remember if there had been a moon last night.

He shook himself into sense. He had to have a plan of campaign. First, he must get out of this room; then he must catch up the column.

He gave the door a resounding kick, but all he managed to do was to crack a toe nail. He wished he had the pair of military boots which the keeper of the horse-change had given him years ago.

Odd that the lever should have fallen like that. It hadn't happened before so far as he could remember; in fact, the lever wasn't normally used. Perhaps it was something to do with the wind and the way the door had slammed.

It was then that he heard the scratching noise. At first he thought that it was one of the mice that lived round the kitchens and came out when everything was quiet to see what they could find. But it wasn't that sort of scratching.

Brutus, maybe? No, it couldn't be Brutus. Brutus never did anything if he could avoid it; but when he did move, he didn't scratch, he pounded. More like parchment being unrolled. Aquilo put his ear to the

26

wall. Parchment meant people. But *what* people? Surely the Saxons couldn't have got here as fast as that? He wanted to shout, but something made him keep silent. Everybody was supposed to have gone. So what was a man doing now in his father's study, unrolling parchment?

More sounds. Different sounds. Banging doors. A squeak.

Aquilo remembered the big wooden chest with bronze corners and bands. It stood in the corner of the study, and his father always kept it locked. But there would be nothing in it now, except the spiders. All the silver, and the gold cups too, would have been packed up to go with the rest of the luggage in the carriage. Vincentius would never leave behind the silver dinner plates with the figure of Mercury engraved on each.

So why was somebody looking?

A sound like something heavy being dragged across the tiled floor. A muttered curse. More scrapings. Footsteps. Then silence.

Aquilo waited a long time, but there were no more sounds from the study. Whoever it was must have gone away. The silence, almost total, made him afraid. The only sound that came to him was the faint murmur of the stream as it escaped over the dam at the end of the mill-race.

Aquilo sat on the bench fixed to the wall and tried to stop his legs shaking. There had always been so many people around the villa, night and day. Yet now there was nobody, nothing.

He went and stood beneath the window, looking up, extending his arms as far as they would go, crooking his fingers ready to grab at the wooden frame. He jumped. The wooden frame came to meet him, eluded

27

his hands, receded. He lay on the floor, wondering whether he had broken anything. One ankle hurt, but not enough to stop him.

He needed something to climb on, and he looked round the shadowy bare room. Just the bedframe, and the bench set against the opposite wall. He limped over to the bench. It would mean breaking the plaster to get it free.

Aquilo applied all his strength to the top bar of the bench. Again he pulled, and the wood moved slightly. A crack appeared in the plaster. In a fury of energy, Aquilo attacked the bench with hands and feet. Splinters tore his hands, but he hardly noticed. Then, with a crash, both terrifying and satisfying, the bench came away from the wall and fell to the floor. Aquilo stood back and gathered his thoughts.

Over to the bed, that's it. Heave it up on top. See it's secure, balanced. Climb.

His hands worked at the wooden shutters over the window. A great gust of cool air filled his lungs and made his eyes smart. He scrambled up. Just in time he remembered the leather bag which contained his knife, plate, and cup. He would need those. He pitched the bag through the window and let it drop to the grass outside. Then he pushed his head out into the night, and wriggled through. The wall was thick, and he was able to sit for a moment before he allowed himself to drop to the thick soft grass beneath.

Quickly he gathered up the bag, slung it over his shoulder, scurried round the corner of the villa to the yard. There was still a hope in the back of his mind that the procession would still be there. His mother would be looking out of the carriage, not allowing them to start till he arrived. But nobody knew he was not with the column or in one of the carts. The yard was empty. The path which led away from the villa towards the high road and the horse-change was deserted.

Not quite empty.

Brutus was still there, his great furry head on his paws. Waiting. Just where he had been told to wait.

Aquilo laughed. His panic had gone. The Saxons were miles away, but the column wasn't. All he had to do was to follow it. It was a mile or two to the horse-change no more.

Aquilo whistled to himself as he picked up Brutus' rope, hauled the dog to his feet, and set off up the gravel road. He could do with a good meal at the horse-change.

He made good time, despite the efforts of Brutus to hinder him. Brutus had had one good long walk that day and after a few yards he sat down in the middle of the road and refused to move. Try as Aquilo might, he could not budge him. He pushed and he pulled, and he yelled 'Food!' at him. Brutus merely twitched one ear as though bothered by a particularly annoying fly, and stayed where he was.

At length in despair he left the rope lying on the road and walked away. The leather bag bumped against him as he walked. He was tempted to abandon it with Brutus, but just as he had almost decided to travel light, he heard great thundering thumps behind him. He looked over his shoulder and grinned. Brutus had fallen for his bluff. Aquilo watched him pounding the gravel beneath his enormous paws, tail flying, tongue lolling, water dripping from his jaws.

Aquilo went down on one knee and gathered the great mass of coarse hair to his chest. The thing to do now was to keep Brutus on the move.

'Come on, boy!' He scrambled to his feet and set off. He turned to see if Brutus was coming, and for the first time noticed the glow in the sky. He stopped, his eyes wide.

The glow was in the eastern sky, a dull orange, rising like a vast moon above the line of the trees. As he watched, it seemed to grow brighter, and then to fade as the smoke billowed up and swallowed it.

It must be three or four miles away, he thought. His first assumption was that the Villa Antiqua was burning, but the glow was too far away, beyond the forest, and in any case there was no sound or smell of burning in the air. Just a destructive light.

The Villa Pulchra. That was it. His father said it had been taken by the Saxons. Perhaps they had found Marcus' store of wine, and drunk too much of it. Perhaps even now they were dancing round their bonfire, brandishing their sparkling swords, their long fair hair streaming in the wind.

And what then?

Tomorrow, or the next day, they would be on the march again. They would be bound to see the Villa Antiqua. The tall tower of the mill would be visible above the tops of the trees, and the long tiled roof would glow red in the sunshine.

Aquilo hurried on. He *must* get to the horse-change before the column left. Brutus lolloped along by his side.

Suddenly the woodland cleared, the road lay open. Long low barns stretched in rigid lines on his left. The flint and brick building on his right, dark and shuttered, sat squat in the night.

Aquilo could hear the stamping of horses, and his heart leapt. But when he ran into the yard, he found it

30

empty. Great solid buildings in a square all round him, cobbles at his feet, a pile of rubbish in one corner, no light.

He shouted. His voice echoed emptily round the walls. He crept silently towards the door of the main building.

A bell, the size of a cooking pot, hung from a frame outside the door. Aquilo had his hand raised to strike it, when he heard the scraping of a key on the inside of the door. He stood back in the shadows.

The door opened, and a small fat man with a completely bald head stood outlined in the dim light which came from a lamp just inside. He held a knife in his hand.

The man was grumbling quietly to himself and swaying from side to side. He put out a short fat arm to steady himself against the doorpost. His head wagged. He was, Aquilo could see, very drunk. Aelian often was.

Brutus had also seen the square of light, and he padded over to find out if there was any possibility of food. He made no sound on the cobbles, and he was nuzzling Aelian's shins before the man was aware of his presence. Aelian let out a string of oaths as he started back, dropping the knife on the doorstep only a yard or two from Aquilo, who stooped to pick it up. Aquilo knew Aelian as a good horse-dealer, though in the last few years business had been bad and he had allowed the establishment to run down.

The light from the door fell on the step and the knife. Something else, small and indistinguishable, shone faintly in the dust, and Aquilo's fingers closed round it. People often dropped coins in the dirt of the yard and couldn't be bothered to look for them. He slipped it into the pouch at his belt, and handed the knife back to the innkeeper.

'Aquilo!' Aelian staggered forward. 'What you want?' The knife made patterns in the air round Aquilo's head.

'My father. Have you seen him?'

'No one comes to my inn any more.'

'But my father must have passed through this evening. Didn't he?' Aquilo could feel the panic rising in his throat.

'No. Nobody. No carriage. Nothing.' Aelian stepped back and began to close the door.

Aquilo tried to squeeze through the crack between the door and the post, but Aelian's great fat fist landed in his chest, and he fell back, clutching at one of the corridor supports.

The door slammed, taking the light away, plunging the cobbled yard into blackness. Aquilo stumbled over the uneven surface. He didn't know where he was going, and he no longer cared.

Chapter Four

He had been walking for a long time. A thin bow of a moon had risen and gave a little light. His feet stumbled over roots and stones, his legs ached.

He was in woods, that much he knew. But the woods stretched for miles on all sides of the Villa Antiqua, creeping over the hillsides like the fur of an animal, with occasional sore spots where the animal had scratched itself for fleas.

He knew he had run from the horse-change, scared and unseeing, with Brutus behind him. After a time he had stopped running, his pace slackening no more than a walk. He had run *away*, but he had nowhere to run *to*.

The villa? It was an empty shell, forlorn, abandoned.

Aquilo stopped and leaned his back against the trunk of a tree. Gradually he sank to the ground, pulling his thick woollen tunic closer round his legs, grateful for the warmth of Brutus lying at his side. A cool breeze had sprung up, sending little ripples of movement through the leaves.

The glow in the sky from the burning villa over the hill was still there, but fainter now. Aquilo's senses snapped together like the leaves of a book. If it *had* been the Villa Pulchra burning in the east, that gave him some idea of direction. He would strike north. In that direction from the Villa Antiqua the country was wild and uninhabited, a landscape of hills and steep valleys with fierce little streams cutting their way through the chalk. The next town was twelve miles to the north, but before that there was the temple, and Vetustus its guardian. He would go to Vetustus.

Now that his mind was made up, Aquilo's confidence returned. The few moments' rest had done him as much good as a whole night's sleep. He got up, slung the leather bag over his shoulder, pulled Brutus to his feet, and marched off. He thought he recognised a glade where the deer used to lie in the heat of the day, and a particular patch of brambles where he had once caught a rabbit.

Before long he reached the road which ran north from the horse-change and followed the ridge of hills. It wasn't much of a road, just a grass track a few paces wide between the tall trees, but it was straight, and its surface felt good to his feet. The grass shone pale in the dim light of the stars and the sickle moon, rippling like a stream running direct to the temple. He would find shelter there. Vetustus would tell him what to do.

He walked along the side of the track, keeping in the shelter of the trees and leaving the rutted middle to the rabbits which played there without fear. Their eyes glowed among the grass.

Suddenly Aquilo came to a halt. He shrank into the bracken, his ears straining, his heart thumping.

A voice. A man's voice among the trees. Singing.

From the covering undergrowth, Aquilo watched and waited. He put a hand over Brutus' nose, but he knew that if the dog was going to bark, nothing would stop him.

The singing came nearer, a strange deep sound. No words.

A crackle of twigs from somebody's feet. Abruptly

34

the singing stopped. Part of the shadows of the tree detached itself and became a man. He wore a long tunic and a fur cloak. A bare sword hung from his belt, and over his shoulder a pole bore a couple of rabbits and a pigeon.

He gave a low whistle. Another tall thick-set figure emerged, similarly dressed.

They exchanged a few words which Aquilo could not understand, and then melted into the woods opposite. The dim light gleamed for a moment on their long fair hair, but then they were gone.

Aquilo cautiously pushed himself free of the bracken and stood up. He knew who they were, these tall fair-haired men. Saxons.

Aquilo stepped into the pale line of the track. He was partly afraid, partly curious. He peered into the shadows of the woods. Long thin black trunks, stretching up to the skies, and between them the faint glow of a fire. Aquilo began to move through the bushes. Brutus padded along behind him.

There was a clearing, the size of the villa yard, and in the middle of it a crackling blaze of dry wood. Flames leapt up, and a column of smoke rose like a ghostly tree, spreading its branches over the glade. Faces gleamed in the firelight. Swords and knives sparkled.

And there was a smell.

Roast deer.

Above the fire was erected an iron spit, held by forked sticks thrust into the ground. Two or three cooking pots hung over the flames, twisting in the heat. The smell was almost something you could touch.

Aquilo was envious. Deer, and rabbits, and pigeons!

These Saxons certainly knew how to look after themselves. He watched through the covering leaves as they worked round the hearth, talking, laughing, singing. Knives cut great pieces of meat as they were ready, leaving the next layer open to the flames. A jug was passed from hand to hand.

After a time, one or two of them lay down by the side of the red-glowing logs and slept, drawing their fur cloaks about them. The rest sat in a ring, talking quietly. One particularly huge man with an enormous white beard and vast hands was carving a model of a boat.

Still Aquilo watched. There was in the back of his mind the idea that perhaps when they had all fallen asleep he might creep into that warm ring and steal some of the food which lay uneaten in pots left carelessly on the blackened grass at the edges of the fire.

Just as well, he thought, that Brutus had gone to sleep. With infinite caution he began to creep out from the cover of the thicket.

The large pot from which the group had been drinking sailed across the fire in his direction, and for one terrified moment he thought he had been seen. But there was somebody else just beyond the thicket, and it was to him that the pot was thrown. A figure moved out into the firelight, clutching the pot to his chest.

A laugh, a shout, an order. The figure with the pot stumbled towards the man with the knife and the model in his huge hands. The man made signs to indicate that the pot was empty and that he wanted it filled.

Aquilo was puzzled. Why did he need to use signs rather than words?

His gaze moved from the huge man to the figure

36

holding the pot. Aquilo could see little except a dirty tunic and a thatch of black hair.

And a rope. A rope, knotted round his neck, and stretching back to a tree.

So he was a prisoner. A slave.

The figure turned to a pile of pots and weapons which lay tumbled at one side of the clearing, and as he did so, Aquilo caught sight of his face.

A cry came welling in his throat, and he managed just in time to hold it in.

Magnus from the Villa Pulchra. Magnus, the son of the owner of the Villa Pulchra.

And now Magnus was a prisoner of the Saxons.

Aquilo watched him as he picked up another jar and took it to the man. When he had put it down by his side, he retreated towards the tree to which the rope round his neck was tied. Aquilo could see his face gleaming in the darkness.

It gave him something to think about. He looked to see that Brutus was still asleep, and then began to crawl round the edge of the clearing to the point where Magnus lay against the tree. His eyes and ears were alert to catch any sign of alarm from the Saxons round the fire, but the man with the knife was busy again with his boat.

He knelt behind the tree. Gradually he slipped one hand round the trunk, feeling the rough bark of it until the tips of his fingers touched the prisoner's mass of hair. Then with one quick movement he clapped his hand over the boy's mouth and brought his head back against the tree.

A log fell in the fire, and the man with the knife looked briefly, kicked it back into place, and went on whittling at the wood in his hand.

Aquilo edged round the tree. The whites of the boy's eyes glittered with fear.

A sudden stab of pain in his hand. Aquilo steeled himself to keep his grip. Magnus couldn't have recognised him, or he wouldn't have used his teeth with such force.

'It's me. Aquilo.'

The boy's tense muscles relaxed, his shoulders sagged.

Aquilo glanced at the group by the fire. He took his hand away from the boy's face, and began to feel for the knot which tied him to the tree.

There it was, a great lump of rope. His fingers tore at the fibres, but after a moment he realised he needed a knife.

'Wait here!' he muttered.

The boy's head moved slightly as he watched Aquilo crawl back into the thicket. Brutus was still lying guard over the leather bag.

Aquilo pulled out the noose round the bag and felt for the knife. When he'd found it he stuck it between his teeth and began to crawl back to Magnus.

Then chance came to help him. The two Saxons still awake, apart from the huge man with the model, had been talking and drinking together, but now whatever it was they were drinking overcame their good temper. In a moment curses had flared into a fight. The knives were out.

Aquilo could see the big man drawing himself to his feet. His white beard shone, and his eyes snapped. He put his vast bulk between the quarrellers and dared them to attack.

'I've nearly cut the rope,' Aquilo murmured to Magnus. 'When I say "go", you go.'

Magnus nodded.

Aquilo sawed at the rope with desperate energy. Would it never give?

The two quarrelling Saxons were circling like dogs round the chief, knives at the ready. The chief's fist shot out, hitting one of them in the chest, knocking him to the ground where he lay gasping.

The rope round the tree finally gave.

'Go!' Aquilo whispered. He could hear the sounds

of Magnus' progress through the grass and dry leaves.

The second Saxon rushed at the chief, but the man with the white beard just stood and received the attack as though he could feel nothing. Aquilo caught a glimpse of his arms raised, the fingers knotted. Then with casual indifference the Saxon chief brought his fists down on the man's head.

Aquilo had reached Brutus by now.

'Come *on*!' he muttered. 'Food!'

Brutus opened one eye, then shambled to his feet, and allowed himself to be pulled through the dark wood, grumbling quietly all the time. The glow of the fire faded behind them.

The grass track opened before them, a silver line leading away into the distance.

They ran.

Chapter Five

'Epona will help you,' Vetustus said, 'if you ask properly.'

'Properly?'

'With all the right ceremonies. I will deal with that.'

Vetustus sat on the doorsill of his hut by the side of the temple. He was an old man, nobody knew how old, for he had been the guardian of the temple ever since anyone could remember. His hair was silver-grey, rough and long, and it joined his beard in a matted tangle. Over his tunic he wore a long cloak of bear-fur, and round his neck hung the image of a rearing horse. It was a bronze horse, its head exaggerated, its nostrils flaring, its eyes a glitter of precious stones, and it thumped against the old man's chest when he moved.

'You must trust Epona. That is all I can tell you. No, perhaps there is more, Aquilo. You must learn the most difficult of all lessons in a strange world – how to survive. Food, drink, shelter – these are the things you must provide for yourself and Magnus.'

'Will he be all right? Magnus, I mean.'

'There is nothing wrong with Magnus that a good night's sleep will not cure. He was tired, that is all.'

Aquilo glanced inside the hut where a dark bundle of rugs and furs covered the sleeping boy. Aquilo was faintly jealous. He was more awake now than he had been all day. He had told Vetustus of all that had happened. He had even told him of the death of the

Brock, though that was a memory he had tried to put at the back of his mind.

He felt safe now. The Old One was a friend. He had proved his friendship many times in the past. He was sitting now, as Aquilo had often seen him, with his back against the wooden post of the hut door, his face wrinkled and wise. Or rather, what you could see of his face. The Old One's head was covered with hair like a shaggy dog's. Only his eyes showed life.

'Well, Aquilo, let me see what you have brought with you to help on your travelling.'

Aquilo obediently emptied the leather bag on the rough stone sill. One bowl, one knife, one cup, a leather bottle, a set of tweezers – and a few crumbs. It wasn't much. Vetustus however thought differently.

'The knife you need. You should keep that in your belt so that it will be ready when you want it. The bowl, yes, a nice piece of pottery. But the cup, Aquilo, do you really need the cup?'

'It's my Mercury cup.'

'Mercury? You had better not let the goddess Epona hear you mention his name. She would be envious. A man must not divide his loyalties.' The Old One's eyes flickered over the stone sill. 'May I see?'

Aquilo handed him the cup. The old man held it close to his eyes, traced the engraving with his finger.

'Ah, I see. Mercury, with his wings and his staff. Mercury is for travellers, and so also is Epona, and that is why she appears in the form of a mighty horse.'

'Like your bronze horse?'

'That is so. Have you seen the goddess herself?'

Aquilo shook his head.

'Perhaps you will. One day, when Epona decides, you will be favoured.'

All the time, the Old One was turning the Mercury cup over and over in his hand, watching the dim light glow on the pewter.

'Yes, a fine piece of work. You must look after it.'

'But you said I could do without it.'

'That was before I saw it. And you have nothing else?'

'Only Brutus, and the rope around his neck.'

'Rope is useful. So is this.' He produced from behind the door a strange device of thin wire and even thinner twine.

'What is it, Old One?'

'You do not know? The rabbits would bless you. A snare, Aquilo. You will need to eat, you know, and nature will not miss a rabbit or two.'

With slow precision, as though he had learnt to use the least possible movement to gain his desire, the old man rose and showed Aquilo how to set the snare.

'You will have to be patient, Aquilo. Rabbits are silly creatures, but they will not run into your snares just when you want them. And when you have caught one, you must prepare it.'

'I've seen that in the kitchen at the Villa Antiqua,' Aquilo replied. 'I know how.'

'Good. And then you must cook it.'

Aquilo remembered the smell of the roasting meat round the Saxon fire. Vetustus had given him bread, and a lump of something which he said was dried meat but tasted like leather.

'Roasting is easy.' he said.

'Yes, if you have the time, and you do not mind letting the whole country know where you are. You see the embers of the fire down there at your feet?'

43

Aquilo looked at the faintly glowing ashes. There was no smoke.

'That will cook for you, Aquilo. It will be safer. Go down to the stream below the temple and bring me two handfuls of the soft clay.'

Aquilo slipped quietly through the trees to the bank of the stream. He felt along the margin till he found the level of orange clay which rested on the chalk. He filled his hands with the soft and yielding substance, and carried it still dripping back to Vetustus.

'Good. Put it down on the stone and roll it out like pastry. You would take your rabbit and wrap it in the clay and put it among the hot ashes. The clay will bake hard, but when you break it open with a stone, dinner will be served. Suppose your cup, your Mercury cup, is the rabbit.' With a few economical movements Vetustus smoothed the wet clay round the cup, inside and out, and then he put it at the edge of the fire. Aquilo was going to pick it out of the glowing embers, but the old man put out a hand to restrain him. 'Perhaps it will be better that way, Aquilo. A disguise. It would be a pity to lose the cup, and somebody seeing the pewter might think it worth stealing, but this mis-shapen clay will excite no one's envy. Keep it safe.'

'I hope Mercury won't mind,' Aquilo said. 'He'll have clay all over his wings.'

'He will have to learn to live with it for a while,' the old man replied shortly. 'Now, what else can we find to fill the night hours?'

Aquilo yawned. It must be very late. Soon he would find a dark corner in the hut and sleep till morning came, but not yet.

'I'd like a curse on whoever made me miss the carriage,' he said. 'And whoever killed the Brock.'

44

'Nothing easier, Aquilo.' Suddenly the old man was all energy. Aquilo could hear him rooting about inside the hut, and then watched through half-closed eyes as he moved to the door of the temple. In a moment he was out again, holding something flat in his hand.

'There we are, Aquilo, all prepared. Now, your curse. What shall it be?'

'I wasn't being serious, Old One.'

'But I was, Aquilo, and I am. A curse it shall be.'

'Will it work, Old One?'

Vetustus laughed. 'You must not let the goddess hear you, Aquilo, or she will turn the curse back upon you.' His teeth flashed in the dimness, and for a moment Aquilo was afraid.

'No, no, that would never do. Now, here is the sheet of lead. You must write on this, and I will curl it up like a shell and give it to Epona, and she will see that the words come true.'

'I don't know what to say.'

'Then I shall say it for you. I shall enjoy it.'

And indeed he did look as though he had been given a special treat, Aquilo thought. There was something magical, ghostly, almost devilish, about the figure wrapped in a bear-hide, with his own grey hair where the bear's muzzle would be. Aquilo pulled the wool blanket which the old man had given him closer round his body, and shrank into the shelter of the shadows. His eyes watched Vetustus' every movement.

The old man's hands passed over the lead sheet. He was muttering to himself, but Aquilo could not make out the words. Suddenly he found the old man's eyes blazing into his.

'Your knife. Give it to me.'

With trembling fingers Aquilo pulled at the knife in

his belt and handed it to Vetustus. The muttering droned on, and the knife glittered in the old man's hand, weaving strange dances across the smooth surface. Gradually the point of the knife moved nearer the lead until the characters began to appear, pictures, strange signs. Then when the writing was finished, the old man sighed, as though he was sorry to have finished. Slowly he began to roll the lead into a thin tube so that the writing could no longer be seen, then he put it on the stone beside him. The knife still glittered in his hand.

He sighed again, glanced at Aquilo, and laughed. 'It is all over, Aquilo. I will see that the roll of lead reaches Epona in the morning. Come, there is no need to look so afraid.'

'I wasn't scared,' Aquilo protested. And he wasn't. Not now.

'No? Tell me, Aquilo, what were you seeing inside your head as I wrote?'

Aquilo's eyes darkened. Then he spoke, and the surprise that he felt was clear in his voice. 'I saw a horse. A great white horse, with flowing mane, and red glowing eyes. It reared up in front of me, until its hooves blotted out the sky.' He stopped. 'I didn't really see that, did I?'

'Epona appears just as you described to those she favours,' Vetustus replied. 'She has been the lady of the chalk hills since time began. Here and there you will see that men have carved her likeness in the face of the downs.'

Suddenly Vetustus shook himself. 'Your knife. You will need it.'

Aquilo pushed the knife into his belt by the side of the pouch which always hung there. 'It's more use

46

than this pouch, anyway. Empty, except for some dice.' A stray memory floated across his mind. 'No, it isn't, though. I found a coin down at the horse-change. Only a little one, but it may buy something.'

'Money now will do you nothing but harm.' Vetustus said. 'Let me see.'

Aquilo felt for the little round object which he had pushed into his pouch at the horse-change. Vetustus held the coin gently between finger and thumb, turned it to catch the light.

'This is no coin, Aquilo.'

'No?' He was disappointed.

'You should look. See! It is the stone of a ring. It has the figure of Mercury carved upon it. Good work, expensive. You say you found it at the horse-change? Some rich man will soon be noticing his loss and asking me, perhaps, for a curse upon the thief.' The old man's eyes twinkled slyly.

Aquilo took the little stone in the palm of his hand. Now that he saw it in the light of a solitary flame which Vetustus had blown into life, he recognised it at once. He had seen it many times on his father's finger, the signet ring with the mark of Mercury. Vincentius always wore it.

Aquilo tried to recall the picture of his father sitting, only that morning, with the bronze box on his knee. His hands were on the lid. If the ring had not been there, or if the stone had been missing, he must surely have noticed its absence.

But he had picked it up that evening at the horse-change.

Aelian, the innkeeper, had said that his father had not been there.

So what was the stone of his ring doing in the horse-change yard?

Something else that Aelian had said came back to his mind. Aquilo had asked the innkeeper if he had seen his father, that was all, but Aelian had said nobody had come that way.

'*Nobody. No carriage.*' Those were his words.

And why should he mention a carriage, unless there *had* been one?'

Chapter Six

Aquilo had been all ready to go racing off to the horse-change at once, but Vetustus advised against it. And for some strange reason Aquilo had suddenly become very sleepy. He fought a battle with his eyelids, but eventually gave it up. Perhaps his sleepiness had something to do with the drink Vetustus gave him.

When he awoke, the sun was already shining. Aquilo scrambled out of the heap of blankets in the corner of the hut and ran outside. He looked at the dew sparkling on the grass, and the bowl of porridge and vegetables on the doorstep.

'You will need that,' a voice told him.

Aquilo glanced up, but he could not see the owner of the voice.

'Vetustus!' he called. 'Where are you?'

'Go to the stream.'

Aquilo ran down to the silvery water. It babbled over a pebble bed until it was lost to view beneath a group of willows.

'You could do with a clean,' a young voice told him disparagingly. It was not Vetustus, and for a few moments Aquilo was puzzled. He had forgotten Magnus. Then he saw him, sitting on the branches of a tree which dipped towards the water. He was trailing his toes in the stream.

'You all right?' Aquilo asked.

'Course I am. I don't scare easily.'

'Seen anyone about?'

'Vetustus up at the temple. And your dog. What's his name?'

'Brutus.'

Magnus threw his leg over the branch and tumbled to the bank. 'You know what happened?'

'At the Villa Pulchra? A bit.'

'They burned it.' Magnus was looking at the stream, and Aquilo could not see his face.

'They burned it,' Magnus repeated. 'They knocked it down, and burned it. That was after the killing.'

Aquilo waited. He had not known Magnus well before, and he had been rather afraid of him when they had met. He was a short thick-set boy, with dark hair and a brown face. He usually scowled, rather than laughed, and he was prepared to fight anyone.

'I don't think anyone escaped except me,' Magnus went on. He looked up from the sun-soaked water, and his eyes blazed. 'I shan't forget them. Ever. The Saxons.'

'The ones who took you prisoner?'

'No, that was another gang. The ones who captured our house are still there, for all I know. They came without warning. I was in the yard at the time, and they came and threw me in the pool. You remember the pool?'

'What happened?'

Magnus shrugged his shoulders. 'It doesn't matter now. I crawled out of the pool by the steps, because that was further away from them. There was the noise of swords as our people began rushing out of the house to fight them off. I wanted to run round the pool and help them, but two hands held me back, and then I heard my uncle say, 'Keep quiet'. So I did. It didn't

50

take long. Our men weren't prepared for it, and they broke and ran, and the Saxons charged in aiming their swords at anything they saw. Then two of them came down the side of the pool towards me.'

Again Magnus stopped for a moment.

'My uncle rushed out at them, but there was nothing he could do. I remember seeing him floating in the pool, with his face in the water. The two Saxons went away then. They were laughing.'

'But you got away?'

'Oh, yes, I got away. I wish I hadn't. I ran and hid and ran again until I could do nothing but lie on the grass and sleep. When I woke up, there was a rope round my neck.'

They had reached the hut now, and sat down to share the bowl of food.

'I've got to find my father, Magnus, and the rest of them.'

Magnus looked at Aquilo over the top of the bowl. 'I will come too.'

'Good,' said Vetustus as he came out of the temple. His silver hair shone in the morning sun. 'I was wondering what to do with the two of you.'

'I'm going to the horse-change,' Aquilo announced. He got up. 'I'm sure that man Aelian knows more than he says.'

'That is one place *not* to go,' Vetustus said. 'A drunkard and an idler. There is no reason why Vincentius should not have kept to his original plan. He will make for Calleva, and from there to Portus, where a boat will take him to Armorica. Sound advice. So you two – '

'Three,' Aquilo interrupted. 'Brutus.'

'You three will take your eight legs to Calleva. But

51

you should avoid the horse-change here. Keep away from the road, and keep your eyes open. Move by hidden paths. Spy out the way before you.'

He broke off. Then, 'Come!' he said. 'I have work to do, even if you have not. I will see you again, perhaps. Aquilo, do not forget the Mercury cup.'

'I won't.'

They packed Aquilo's leather bag with the food which Vetustus gave them, then walked down to the stream. The old man watched them from the door of the temple. It was nothing more than a square hut with a corridor all round it built on posts, but it looked safe and comfortable.

They walked all morning, although it took all Aquilo's efforts to keep Brutus going. The sun was almost at its highest when Aquilo took pity on him. They sat in the shade of an enormous oak, eating bread and cheese. There was an onion as well, to add a little flavour, and a curious sort of leaf which looked like nothing Aquilo had ever seen before, but tasted vaguely of mint.

'What about Brutus?' Magnus said when they had finished. The sun was making patterns through the branches of the oak on the grass beneath, and the flies were dancing in the bright rays like drunk slaves after harvest. It was very quiet.

Aquilo laid one hand on the dog's head and felt for the place behind his ears where he knew Brutus loved being rubbed.

'I don't know,' he said uncertainly. 'He's never had to look after himself before. That lump of bread we gave him won't last him long.'

'He'll have to learn.' Magnus sounded very sure. His dark eyes were almost closed, but Aquilo could see that all his senses were alert. They had met no one so far, but they had kept away from the road.

'Learn to catch things for himself? Old Brutus?'

'It's either that, or dying,' Magnus said. 'How far do we have to go?'

'To Calleva? About fifty miles, I suppose. There's a lot of hills in between. And then the great river as well.'

'Have you ever been that far?'

'No.'

'Fifty miles. Still, there will be towns and farms before that. We shall find food. We shall have to.' He sounded very determined. Aquilo suddenly realised that Magnus was concentrating his mind on the journey because he needed to blot out the thought of what had happened at the Villa Pulchra.

'How many of the fifty have we done so far?' Magnus went on.

'Ten perhaps.'

'So, another ten before nightfall, perhaps more, if we keep going. We might even be at Calleva tomorrow night. Do you know that your people will be there?'

Aquilo shook his head, and the flies buzzed. He was thinking of the Brock, and the knife in the Brock's chest. One day he'd find out who had done that, and take vengeance.

They left the clearing under the tree with Brutus padding along behind them. He was feeling the heat, and for his sake Aquilo tried to ease their pace, but Magnus' face was set firmly southwards.

'Your legs must be made of iron,' Aquilo told him.

'Then it is better to wear them out, rather than let them rust,' was all the answer he got.

About the middle of the afternoon they skirted

round another horse-change. There were some carts with thick solid wheels in the yard, and a few horses running in the paddock at the back, but no sign of the big carriage belonging to Vincentius.

'We could take two of those horses,' Aquilo suggested.

'And have them after us at once?' Magnus growled. 'Anyway, you'd never get Brutus on a horse. We can trust our own feet. Come on!'

Aquilo sat down to inspect the back of his heels. The leather of his sandals was beginning to rub a sore patch. He took them off and pushed them into his bag. Magnus didn't seem to notice. He strode on with hardly a backward glance.

Suddenly they were looking at a villa. The trees thinned and fields opened on a hillside bright in the setting sun. They dropped to their knees and watched from behind a gorsebush.

'We'll work our way round by that hedge,' Magnus said, 'You see the second field? It's a lower level than this one. There'll be a ditch, and plenty of cover.' He began to move stealthily towards the corner of the hedge. Aquilo followed him, hauling Brutus behind him.

It was Brutus who gave the first warning of danger. A short bark, and an enquiring look at his master. But Aquilo had no time to notice why Brutus was hanging back. He pulled at the rope with irritation: it was bad enough Magnus rushing ahead without bothering to look to see if he was following. He'd better catch him up before he turned the corner at the end of the field.

Magnus disappeared, and Aquilo hurried on, ignoring Brutus' snuffles of alarm.

With a rush he reached the corner. Magnus was not

far away, just a few paces. He was fighting furiously against a man who was trying to pinion his arms and ward off Magnus' fists at the same time. Brutus leapt forward, pulling Aquilo with him.

Chapter Seven

It was not until Brutus stopped barking and began to roll on the ground in front of the man, that Aquilo realised who it was.

'Am I glad to see you!' he exclaimed.

The man looked up, still trying to fend off Magnus' wild attack.

'Aquilo!' he said. 'Tell this young whirlwind to calm down.'

'It's all right, Magnus! Leave him alone!' Aquilo rushed through the windmill of Magnus' fists. 'It's Felix.'

Magnus dropped his arms. His expression was still wary, but there was doubt in his dark eyes.

'It's my father's steward. He's a friend.'

Magnus slipped from Felix' grasp and stood a pace or two away, glowering from under dark eyebrows.

'I was hoping you would come this way,' Felix said. 'I'll say one thing for your friend. He knows how to make his fists felt.' He began to rub his chin. There was a small trickle of blood coming from a cut at the corner of his mouth.

'Where's my father?' Aquilo demanded. 'How far has he got?'

'There was a change of plan. A message came that the road was filled with a band of escaped slaves from further south, so Vincentius changed his mind.'

Aquilo sat down on the edge of the ditch. All his energy had gone. Brutus put his head on Aquilo's knee. His big brown eyes looked hopefully up at him. Aquilo absently pulled at the dog's ears.

'Where *is* he going, then?'

'To Aquae Sulis.'

'But that's in the west.'

'And that's why I am here. You see, after the message came and Vincentius decided to go to Aquae, we took the western road, leaving the horse-change without stopping, and it wasn't until we'd gone some miles that we realised you were missing. I offered to come and fetch you. It was likely that you would be on the road to Calleva. Fortunately I saw you coming down the hillside. It was your white hair, Aquilo, that gave you away. I almost thought it was a Saxon head at first.'

'So we've got to go back,' Magnus said. Without another word he began to march off by the line of the ditch.

'There's no hurry,' Felix said. 'Come back here, young sir, unless you prefer to walk rather than ride.'

Magnus stopped. 'Ride?'

'I have two horses and a chariot. How do you think I got here so fast? I borrowed the chariot from the horse-change. Nobody seemed to mind.'

Felix led them to the yard of the villa. It looked deserted, abandoned. Aquilo went up the steps to the corridor and shouted, but there was no answer.

'They packed up and went a few years back,' Felix called up to him. 'So you won't be disturbing anyone.'

Aquilo pushed open one of the doors. It was hanging on one hinge, and it scraped on the floor. It was a beautifully laid mosaic floor, a picture of the four seasons with borders of twisted rope and twining vine-leaves, but somebody had built a rough fire in the middle of it.

Magnus was looking over his shoulder.

'We had one like that,' he said. 'But it had a red and yellow lion in the middle. I always liked that lion.' He turned away.

Felix was busy in the yard preparing the chariot. It was one of the light ones, intended for no more than one messenger, but it looked sturdy enough despite the worn iron on its wheels and the dents in the bronze decorations round the side.

'It's seen a bit of service,' Aquilo said.

They climbed onto the small platform. It was no more than a pace from one side to the other, rounded at the front and straight at the back, but there was just enough room for the three of them and Brutus. The dog didn't at all like the swaying motion and the bumps and the rattles, but he eventually lay down at Aquilo's feet and grumbled unhappily to himself.

The horses lumbered out of the cobbled yard and turned into the road. Felix cracked his whip, and they were away, clinging to the sides, bending their knees to the sway, feeling the cool wind of evening in their faces.

'How long will it take?' Aquilo jerked out. It seemed to him that, with the furious pace Felix was setting, the carriage they were trying to catch up might be just round the next bend.

'An hour or two, perhaps three.'

'All the way to Aquae?'

'No. We shall not do that tonight. It will be dark soon. We can put up at the horse-change. We shall need food, and you two could do with some sleep. There might even be a good meal for Brutus.'

The dog momentarily lifted his head from his paws as he heard his name. His eyes were on Aquilo. Aquilo was thinking. He did not at all like the idea of going back to the horse-change where Aelian would probably still be drunk. He glanced at Felix. All he could see of him was a broad back and a great mass of black hair, but it looked reassuring.

It was dark when they reached the horse-change. Aquilo and Magnus helped Felix with the horses.

A little wavering light bobbed at them from across the yard. Aelian *was* drunk, but at least he seemed to be in a better temper. His face was all smiles, and his bald head was sticky with sweat.

'If it isn't master Aquilo! Welcome to my humble roof!'

Aquilo stepped smartly back, and Brutus growled, but that was because Aquilo had trodden on him.

'Come along inside. You must be hungry, I'm sure. Felix, bring them in, the poor dears.' His little fat hands clutched the candle he was carrying as though it was something precious.

Magnus pulled Aquilo's arm and muttered, 'Is he all right?'

'Just drunk,' Aquilo said. 'It's usual.'

It was filthy inside, and it smelled of bad wine and sweat. A fire was struggling to keep alive on the hearth where a black iron pot hung on a hook. Two earthenware lamps were burning on the rough-hewn table, their untended wicks producing more smoke than light.

Magnus sat in a dark corner, almost invisible. It was plain from his eyes which followed every movement that he trusted nobody.

Brutus made straight for the fire.

'There's a good dog!' Aelian spluttered, as much oil dripping from his voice as did from the lamps. 'Food.'

59

Brutus would have followed anyone who said that to him. Aelian placed a wooden bowl in front of him, full of something red and moist. It smelled dreadful, but Brutus wolfed it down in no time at all.

There was food on the table, bowls of some sort of stew from the pot on the hearth, and great hunks of bread. Aquilo was almost as hungry as Brutus, and he sat at the table opposite Felix, too busy for mere words.

'Won't your friend have supper?' Aelian enquired, rubbing his fat hands together.

Gradually Magnus moved towards the table, and almost against his will took the stool which Aelian offered. He ate, but his eyes were still wary.

'You will have the best room,' Aelian said when supper was over. 'No, no payment. I am glad to serve the son of Vincentius.'

They followed the fat oily little man along the corridor to a big square room at the end. It was plain and bare, what they could see of it in the light of one lamp, and the floor hadn't been swept for a long time. There was a smell like dead rats. A pile of mattresses stuffed with straw lay in one corner. Magnus pulled one out and tested it for comfort.

'If this is his best room,' he said, 'I'd hate to see the others. Here, this one isn't too bad. Where's Brutus?'

'Lying across the door.'

'Good. I don't trust that fat lump of grease.'

Aquilo took the lamp over to the door and examined the latch. 'There's no lock,' he said. 'Still, Brutus will tell us if anyone comes.'

'If he wakes up.' Magnus didn't sound convinced.

'We can pile all the rest of the mattresses against it,' Aquilo suggested. 'At least, that will hold a burglar up a bit.'

'Burglar?' Magnus snorted. 'Murderer, more like.' He began piling mattresses against the door. Brutus thought this was entirely for his benefit and stretched himself out on top of them, gave one long shuddering yawn, and was almost immediately asleep.

Aquilo lay looking at the stars in the square window. He was tired, but sleep did not come at once. He could hear voices from the room along the corridor, shouts of laughter, the occasional snatch of song. Aelian had opened another jar of wine.

Mercury was in Aquilo's mind. A tall figure, slim, with winged sandals and a winged hat, beckoning to him with his twisted staff. He was saying something, but his mouth was full of clay and no words could be distinguished.

Suddenly Aquilo was awake. His leather bag, where was it? He had left it in the kitchen where they had eaten. He got up and moved to the pile of mattresses.

He was drawn by the sound of voices. He thought he could hear the name Mercury, but perhaps that was still inside his head, part of his dream.

Aelian was sitting at the table. He was drinking from a wine jug without bothering to pour it into a cup. There was a pottery lamp on the table, a heap of dirty bowls, and the leather bag.

'I came for my things,' Aquilo said.

Aelian spun round, so startled that he fell to his knees on the filthy floor. 'You scared me, master Aquilo.' He managed a greasy chuckle.

'My things,' Aquilo said. 'On the table.'

'I was just looking to see if everything was in order, master Aquilo. Just to help you, you see.'

Aquilo didn't bother to say anything. He marched to the table, looked inside the bag, noted the bowl, the

61

cup with its covering of clay, the linen bundle which contained the crumbs of the food Vetustus had given them.

Aquilo went back to the room at the end of the corridor. Thoughtfully he pushed the mattresses back into place. Brutus was still grumbling in his sleep, but Magnus had not even noticed. Aquilo lay down.

Epona was in his head now. A great horse with flaming eyes, rearing up on its hind legs, snorting and whinnying. There was something terrible about Epona, something mysterious, ghostly. The horse filled his brain with its power and fury. It reared again, and flame belched from its mouth and its nostrils. Bitter smoke seemed to choke Aquilo's lungs, to fill his eyes so that water streamed from them, but still the flames leapt and writhed. He tried to rub the smoke out of his eyes, and he drew one great gulping breath.

His eyes were open now, and he could see.

The flames were real.

Chapter Eight

It took Aquilo only a moment to race to the door and begin to haul the pile of old mattresses away. He was thinking all the time of Aelian, the drunken old fool Aelian, and the lamp he had probably knocked over. He yelled to Magnus, but found he was already beside him, pulling at the heap of blazing straw. The room was full of black choking smoke.

Aquilo jerked the door open and ran out into the corridor. The floor came up to meet him, and he realised he was on all fours, crawling. He clawed at the wall. His arms were suddenly full of panic-stricken fur, Brutus' tongue was licking his face, and Brutus' paws were scrabbling at his chest. Magnus crashed into him from behind, and they rolled together down the steps to the yard. At the bottom they landed on something soft which Aquilo recognised as Aelian.

'Is he dead?' Magnus muttered.

'No. Just *out*.'

Aelian's fat hands surrounded the neck of the jug, clutching it to his chest. He seemed unaware that the wine was slowly dribbling over his shoulder.

Aquilo turned to look at the blaze.

'We'll have to do something, or the whole place will go,' he gasped.

'Does it matter?' Magnus said. He was looking down at the slack figure of Aelian with contempt in his eyes.

'Course it does. Where's Felix?'

They shouted his name, but there was no reply above the crackling of the flames.

'The horses!' Aquilo suddenly yelled. He raced to the stable block which was one whole side of the yard, and began unlatching the doors. The few horses that were there were nervous, restless, aware of the smoke in their nostrils, inclined to kick. He tore at the ropes which tied the horses to their stalls. The dream of the rearing horse with the flaring eyes was still in his mind. It was the dream which had saved him from the fire, and in some strange way he felt that Epona, the goddess of the horse, was helping him.

There were only five horses all told. He led them out and turned them loose through the gate into the paddock where they usually grazed by day. Then he ran back for a bucket he had noticed lying in the corner. Magnus had had the same idea and was already at the well-head which stood at the end of the yard.

They took a bucket each and raced along the corridor to try and douse the flames. Orange tongues were licking at the door at the end, but two full buckets dealt with them.

'Heave those mattresses over the edge into the yard!' Magnus bellowed.

The wind in the yard made the flames leap and dance as mattress after mattress was added to the heap on the cobbles. There were no flames now in the room at the end.

They stood and watched the bonfire.

'We were lucky,' Aquilo said.

'Yes.' Magnus was holding his hands to the fire as though this was some sort of party. The light flickered on his dark hair and shining eyes. 'Hasn't it occurred to you?'

'What?'

'The fire. There was no big blaze in the kitchen. Just those mattresses.'

Aquilo watched the sparks flying upwards. A sudden thought struck him. 'Shan't be a moment,' he said, and ran up the steps. Magnus could see him looking into all the rooms along the corridor, could hear him calling for Felix. Aquilo came back swinging his leather bag over his shoulder.

'I've rescued this, anyway, but I can't find Felix anywhere. Perhaps he's gone off to the villa to get supplies – that's the most likely thing.'

'Perhaps.' Magnus was still brooding over the fire. The flames were beginning to die down now. 'It was only the mattresses that were on fire,' he said.

Aquilo suddenly realised what he was talking about.

'And we had one lamp, but I remember putting that out, so it wasn't us. And the mattresses were inside the room.'

Aquilo was silent. He stared into the heart of the fire, thinking. If it hadn't been for Epona in his dreams, they'd both be dead now. Odd that Epona should take that much trouble. It ought to have been Mercury.

Mercury!

He had heard Aelian talking about Mercury. He had found Aelian with the bag in front of him. What had he been looking for? The only thing he had of any value was the Mercury cup, but even that was only pewter. Aelian hadn't recognised it in its coating of half-baked clay. And why should Aelian *want* to steal a pewter cup with an engraving of Mercury?

Aquilo clutched the bag to him. He glanced over his shoulder into the dark corner where the innkeeper lay, but he could no longer make out his shape.

'He's gone!' he shouted. 'Aelian's gone!'

'What?' Magnus' eyes darted round the square yard, lit only by the remains of the fire and the thin crescent of the moon. Part of the black outline which was the chariot detached itself and became a round wavering figure. Something bright gleamed in Aelian's hand.

'Look out!' Magnus shouted. 'He's got a knife!'

Aquilo gave one appalled look at Aelian and ran for the cover of the fire. The fat innkeeper waddled after him. His progress was a series of lurches from side to side, and it might have been funny if it had not been for the knife.

Aquilo's eyes were fixed fast on that glittering tongue of polished iron. He wanted to move, to run, to escape, but his legs refused to budge.

Aelian was only a pace or two away now, and still Aquilo stood. He was aware of someone shouting behind him, and he had time to think that it was Magnus. He wished Felix would come back.

An abrupt explosion of noise broke the stillness.

Brutus, cowering in the shadows, had seen Aelian's unsteady advance. He launched himself at the man's chest, growling, worrying the coarse wool tunic. His attack broke the spell which had held Aquilo immobilised.

He shouted to Magnus, and together they raced for the gate which led to the road. Aquilo glanced back. Aelian was a round heap of oaths and yells, rolling in the mud. The knife lay on the ground.

Brutus came loping up. Aquilo seized the rope which trailed from his neck, and throwing the leather bag over his arm, he ran for all he was worth. When

the horse-change had disappeared in the dark, he stopped beneath a clump of trees to get his breath back.

'I told you we couldn't trust him,' Magnus panted.

Aquilo's gaze was on the road. Would there be any pursuit? That depended on how drunk Aelian was. For once, Magnus seemed to have nothing to suggest. He was sitting on his haunches, with his back to a tree.

Aquilo forced his brain to think. 'We can't stay here,' he said. 'The temple.'

Magnus' head jerked up. 'The Old One of the woods?'

'It would be safe for the night, and tomorrow we can start on the western road.'

'All right.' Magnus pulled himself wearily to his feet.

It was dark under the trees. The thin moonlight hardly pierced the dense canopy of leaves. They passed the Villa Antiqua, dark and unwelcoming, and began to climb the hills beyond.

They had been walking an hour when doubt began to creep into his mind. The glades and patches of scrubby woodland were unfamiliar. Trees stood motionless in the still night air, silver and black columns of a natural temple. But of the straight lines of Vetustus' temple there was no sign.

Some of Aquilo's doubt reached Magnus.

'How far to go?' he grunted, as they stood at the top of a bare hill, looking down at a dark and silent valley.

'Not far. If we can get to the stream, we shall know the way better.'

A wide hillside opened before them. A line of trees stood like sentinels along the top, and away in the distance a river gleamed, but it was wider than the stream which bubbled by Vetustus' temple.

They were walking between mounds of earth, the height of a man and three times as wide. Groups of mounds made patterns on the still hillside, their shadows as black as charcoal.

Suddenly Magnus stopped. Aquilo looked back and saw that his eyes were wide in the moonlight and his face white.

'I know this place, Aquilo,' he said in a whisper. 'I came here once when I was small. The slave who was meant to be looking after me got into trouble for letting me wander too far. I never came again until now.'

'Why?'

'The local people call it the valley of the tombs. For centuries their chiefs and elders were buried here. No one ever comes now. No one. It is for the dead alone.'

Aquilo pulled Brutus closer to him. His eyes darted along the lines of earth mounds, down towards the gleaming river.

His body stiffened. His gaze concentrated on one group of mounds just to their right. Magnus followed his pointing finger, and Aquilo heard him catch his breath in sudden panic.

Somebody was moving in the shadows.

Chapter Nine

Aquilo and Magnus drew back into the shelter of one of the mounds. Aquilo's heart was pounding in his chest, and his breath came in bursts which sounded to him like a horse's hooves on a stone road.

It was a thin figure, dressed in something white and flowing. She held a staff in one hand with which she guided her footsteps among the dark earth mounds. Moonlight shone on long pale hair. Gold gleamed at her neck and at her wrists.

She was quite close to them before she stopped.

'Who are you?' Her voice was soft, low, beautiful. 'Tell me.'

Aquilo tried to shrink even further back to escape notice, but Brutus was curious. He pulled Aquilo out from the mound, sniffing and slobbering as he usually did when he met anyone new. Aquilo watched with wonder.

'You need have no fear.'

'I'm not afraid,' Magnus said stoutly, coming out into the open.

The girl turned her fair head towards him.

'There are two of you? You have names?'

'Mine is Aquilo,' Aquilo said, half embarrassed.

'Then you will be as dark as the north wind, is that so?'

'Well, no,' Aquilo replied. He stopped. He had suddenly realised that the girl was blind. 'That doesn't matter, anyway. My name's always been a sort of joke.

There are two of us, though. The other one's called Magnus.'

'And is he one of the great ones?' There was almost a laugh in the girl's voice.

'We're lost,' Aquilo blurted out.

'That I know. Nobody would come here in the middle of the night because he wanted to do so. Come here, Aquilo.'

She lifted one hand and ran it lightly over his head and shoulders.

'Now I shall know you again, Aquilo. Why are you running away?'

The question startled him. 'How did you know?'

'Those who cannot see have other ways. Where will you go?'

'I don't know. We were making for the temple. Can you tell us how to get there?'

'You will not reach the temple tonight. Wait for the sunrise, Aquilo. I am quite harmless. I will take you to my father. He cannot speak, but he can see.'

'Is it far?'

'No more than a few paces. You will come?' She held out her hand, and Aquilo allowed himself to be led.

They came to a deep dell in which the moonlight lay like a liquid blanket. In the middle of it rose a mound, longer than the others they had passed, with two arms extending towards the river and enclosing a black entrance. The arms seemed to close round them, blotting out the light.

'Have no fear,' the girl urged.

'I can't *see*,' Aquilo complained. His feet were dragging on loose flints.

A door had opened in front of him, and he found

71

himself staring at a small square room, low-ceilinged,
lit by one candle set on a stone shelf. On another block
of stone, seat-high, a man perched, his legs tucked
under him. They could not see his face, for his head
was bent over parchment and pens, and he was
writing, slowly, methodically.

'It is I, father. I have brought guests.'

The man's hands became motionless, his head
stayed bowed.

Aquilo looked at the stone floor, the great slabs of
stone which made the walls, the single block of stone

which was the roof. It was cold, with a bitterness he had not known since the winter years ago when the earth had been frozen for two months together. He felt attracted towards the flame of the candle, like a moth in the darkness of the night.

The girl's laughter filled the stone cavern. 'Come in, Magnus. There is milk, and bread, and apples. Are you hungry?' She sat curled up in a corner on another stone shelf with Brutus at her feet.

The man with his back to the room was as still as stone. The girl had said he could not speak. Why not?

Aquilo stared at the thin figure, mis-shapen by the light from the candle, its shadow even more monstrous on the walls and roof. The shadow moved, but the man did not.

The girl's soft voice was in Aquilo's head.

'My father knows what it is to be in danger, and so do I. Perhaps my words will help you. Think of the cup with the winged carving.'

'My Mercury cup?'

'Winged sandals and a winged hat. The staff points down to the earth beneath the feet. Remember the staff, Aquilo. It points in the direction you must go.'

'But I don't understand – ' Aquilo began, but the girl continued as though he had said nothing.

'Men with long fair hair will stand in your way. You must fight them by being one of them, as pale as they are, as strong of heart. You will understand.'

Aquilo sat with a crust of bread in his hand, looking at the girl as she leaned against the stone wall, her long white clothing covering even her feet.

'Why?' Magnus suddenly looked up. 'Why do you live here?'

'I have never known another home,' the girl said

simply. Her lips did not seem to be moving, but the voice was hers. 'When I was no more than a year old, beasts of the forest came to the hut where we lived. Wolves howled in the depth of winter. I lay near the fire one night when the snow drove against the walls. One wolf almost had me in its mouth.'

'And now you are blind?'

'Now I am blind. My father is my eyes, and I am his tongue.'

Again Aquilo's gaze turned to the still figure with his back to him.

'My father fought the wolves and drove them away. I know he has the scars upon his face, but I cannot see them.'

The girl's laughter crept into Aquilo's brain. He looked at her long hair and her white dress, and at the staff which stood by her side, propped against the wall. She could not see, but she laughed.

Aquilo was tired. His eyelids wanted to close, his head to fall on his chest, but he forced himself to stay awake. He could see Magnus opposite, almost asleep as he sat. He struggled against the hot tempest of exhaustion which blew across the deserts of his brain. He knew that she had said words which he must keep in his memory, but he felt them already slipping away from his grasp. He tried to make his legs stand, but he knew that not a muscle moved. The cold of the stone floor reached to his bones, froze the will to action.

Was that why the girl laughed?

He was falling asleep, and he knew that there was nothing he could do to prevent it. He would sleep. Perhaps for ever.

He must escape from this stone tomb before its iciness made him like itself. His eyes searched the walls, his fingers clawed at the stone. Or was it that he only thought they did, because that was what he wanted, while his body lay on the ground incapable of movement? He could almost watch himself and his own futility, as though from another body.

Was that, too, why the girl laughed? The sound was like the running of a stream drenched in moonlight.

He had to make one last effort. He had to stand, to run, to find refuge.

The door was open wide, and the darkness beyond like a thick curtain. He grasped the stone doorpost and called desperately to Magnus, but Magnus made no movement. He staggered towards Magnus' inert body, grabbed him by the shoulders, heard his muscles crack with the strain.

The cold air played on his forehead. The great earth arms towered above him, leaving only a thin strip of sparkling stars. He ran back for Brutus. The rope lay across the stone floor.

He thought he saw the girl's arm raised, but it was not directed at him. His gaze was drawn to the staff by her side. The shadows from the candle fluttered about her hands so that the staff seemed to have wings.

'*Remember the staff, Aquilo.*' He heard himself repeat the girl's words, but they made no sense in his head.

The man who had been writing still sat by the stone ledge. As Aquilo watched the flickering candle, the shadow of the man began to move, to grow larger, to fill the stone tomb with its own darkness. Slowly the figure turned so that it looked at the doorway, at Aquilo.

Then it was that Aquilo knew why he could not speak. The mark of the wolf was upon him. No man

who bore such marks would ever speak again. A face must have lips and teeth and tongue to speak. He had none.

With a cry of terror Aquilo flung himself away from the stone tomb. The blackness of the shadow closed round about him, and he fell into the deep pit of the night.

Chapter Ten

The light of morning shone upon Aquilo's face. He opened his eyes, and was for the moment disconcerted by the grass. The field with its groups of earth mounds lay all around him, and though there were shadows cast by the sun, they were no longer things of terror.

He ran down to the river. The water, swift-running and clear, was cold to his legs, his arms, his face. Schools of little fish, each no more than an inch long, darted among the reeds, changing course in perfect time like soldiers under orders.

Magnus came and stood by his side. Aquilo glanced up.

'I've brought your bag,' Magnus said, dumping it beside him. 'And if you think you're clean, you're not.'

Aquilo received a sudden push in the back from Magnus' foot. The river came up to hit him, and he was spluttering, gasping for breath, his hands beating the water, his feet trying to find a purchase in the mud.

When he looked again, Magnus was sitting on the bank. His face was still an expressionless mask. One leg was dangling in the river, the other drawn up to his chin.

Aquilo stood in the middle of the river, pushing the wet hair out of his eyes.

'Watch out!' he called. 'There's Brutus just behind you!'

Magnus momentarily looked over his shoulder, and Aquilo dived for the dangling leg. Magnus yelled, but his yells soon became nothing more than gurgles. Aquilo climbed onto the bank.

They lay in the grass waiting for the sun to dry their wet tunics on them. Purple thistles stood in ranks all round them, cutting out the sight of everything except a patch of blue sky where a skylark no more than a tiny speck, hung in the air, singing and singing.

'Magnus,' Aquilo said, 'did it really happen?'

'What?'

'Last night.'

Magnus suddenly sat up. 'There's a kingfisher over there. Look!' A flash of bright colour streaked across the water.

Aquilo sighed. Words were running through his head.

'Ask your father what he was doing up at the temple in the middle of the night.'

That had been the Brock, just before he was killed. Somebody had put a knife into his chest. Why?

'Remember the staff. The staff points down to the earth beneath the feet.'

Aquilo idly wiggled his toes. His wet sandals were by his side, steaming in the morning heat. The words went round in his head like the sails of a creaking windmill.

He sat up. There ought to be the crumbs of something edible in his bag. He pulled it towards him, loosening the leather thong, and diving his hand into its rough interior. A hunk of hard bread. Well, it was better than nothing. He couldn't remember putting it there, but it was food.

He gave some to Magnus, and began to chew his own share. He emptied the bag onto the ground, just in case he had missed something. There was the bowl, the odds and ends, the clay-covered cup, the snare Vetustus had given him.

'We'll have to use that,' Magnus said.

Aquilo thought of the long journey to the west. How far would his parents have gone by now? Perhaps they would already be at Aquae Sulis, waiting for him, perhaps even giving up hope. He scrambled the things back into the bag.

'You ought to wash that cup,' Magnus advised.

Aquilo held the cup in his hands. The half-baked clay was cracked and blackened. He began to pick at the roughnesses with his nails, then he stopped.

'No,' he said. 'It's the only valuable thing I've got. It's better hidden.'

They began the long haul up the hillside, Aquilo and Magnus, and Brutus pulling on the rope. They skirted to one side of the earth mounds, because it was easier rather than because there was any sense of fear attached to them now.

Aquilo had no exact plan. All he knew was that he must follow the sun westwards. It was with some surprise that they found themselves on the green road which led north from the Villa Antiqua. Aquilo recognised it almost at once.

'North, south, or west?' Magnus demanded.

'We ought to find Felix,' Aquilo said doubtfully.

'But if he's going to the west, then that is the way we should go too. To Aquae.'

'We *were* going to Vetustus,' Aquilo pointed out, 'before we lost our way in the dark last night.'

'That is north. Out of the way.'

'But Vetustus always knows everything. He probably knows where Felix is. Only a mile or two.'

'A mile or two might make all the difference.'

Aquilo made up his mind. 'I'm going north, to the temple,' he said. 'Come on!' He marched off up the green road, and he had gone some way before he realised that Magnus was not with him. He turned. Magnus was standing in the middle of the road, not moving.

Aquilo stared. All his life decisions had been made for him. His parents had always thought of him as too young to decide for himself, and in any case, they had been too busy to notice that he was no longer a baby.

Well, he had made a decision now. He was going to the temple, and he was not going to change his mind.

'All right,' he called out, and waved. He pulled Brutus' rope, swung the leather bag over his shoulder, and walked on.

He had gone no more than a hundred paces when he realised that Magnus had caught him up. Nothing was said.

Now that he knew where he was, his confidence increased. He was even whistling as he strode along.

'As soon as we get to Vetustus,' he said, 'everything will be all right.'

The clearing in which the temple stood, looking west over the plain, was quiet and deserted. Nobody answered Aquilo's call. A deer which had been browsing down by the stream lifted its head, scented them, scampered away with a scattering of broken twigs. A single bird screamed.

For one moment Aquilo thought that perhaps the band of Saxons had discovered the temple, taken Vetustus prisoner, even killed him, perhaps were still there, lurking behind the trees, ready to pounce. His eyes flashed round, alarmed, but there was no movement. Brutus had flopped down in front of the little round hut where Vetustus lived.

'Well?' Magnus asked.

'He can't be far away,' Aquilo said, trying to sound cheerful. 'He never is. Gone looking for food, I should think.'

'Not a bad plan,' Magnus commented. He wandered off down to the stream, leaving Aquilo standing alone in the clearing.

Aquilo sat on the stone step of the hut and waited. It was not for some time that he noticed the stick in the ground. It was carved like the stick which Vetustus often carried, with the rough representation of a horse's head at the top. There was a curious arrangement of white stones round its base.

'The staff points down to the earth beneath the feet,' he heard himself say aloud.

Then his eyes opened wide. The stones at the base of the stick, he now saw, were arranged in the shape of an arrowhead: the letter V, for Vetustus. And the tip of the arrow pointed to the stream.

He got up and went to look for Magnus. He couldn't find him at first, for he was lying on his front by the bank, looking down into the cool waters. His hands were busy below the surface of the stream. It looked almost as though he was stroking the water, but as Aquilo looked more closely over his shoulder, he could see the sleek shape of a fish.

Suddenly with a splash and a commotion the fish was in Magnus' grasp, was in the air, was lying flapping on the grass, where another fish already lay.

Magnus got up and dusted his knees. There was a

look of quiet triumph in his eyes, though he certainly didn't smile.

'Food,' he said laconically. 'Is there a fire up there?'

'The remains of one.'

Magnus marched up the hill and was soon busy in the hut, blowing the embers of the fire into a blaze.

'Vetustus is somewhere around,' Aquilo said as he watched him. 'He left this sign, so he'll be back soon.'

Magnus glanced up. 'I noticed that,' he said.

The fish were very good. Aquilo was even prepared to say so. They had nearly finished when Aquilo realised that Vetustus was standing at the edge of the clearing. The Old One's teeth gleamed for a moment in the midst of his grey beard. 'You have left some for me?'

'Well, not much.'

'The fish from my stream are good, then?'

Magnus looked up quickly, suspicion in his face.

'How did you know it was fish?'

Again the gleam of teeth.

'Magnus, an old man's senses do not completely wither I can still use my nose. I expected you, Aquilo.'

'I saw your stick, and the arrowhead.'

'I have been gathering news, Aquilo. The country is full of rumour, but I do not know how much is true and how much false.'

'Have you heard about my parents, Old one?'

'Yes.'

'Which way did they go? To Aquae?'

'Aquilo, I do not know.' Vetustus sat on the step in the sun. 'I have a message for you.'

'From Felix?'

'From Felix. You are to meet him at the Villa Antiqua at nightfall tonight.'

It was a long day. Vetustus was busy about the temple, though Aquilo never quite knew where he might be at any one time. He seemed to be able to move through the woodland without disturbing a single leaf.

Aquilo and Magnus tried to catch a rabbit in the snare, but, as Magnus pointed out, it was the wrong time of day. At any rate, their efforts met with no success. Brutus startled himself by finding what he thought was a rabbit hole. He stuck his nose into it and his front paws scrabbled at the loose earth. There was no rabbit in the hole, only a nest of wasps.

As the sun began to set across the stream, turning the water to gold, they again sat on the stone step, eating bread and the little green apples which looked sour but were surprisingly sweet.

The thought of the Brock, killed in the sunshine at the Villa Antiqua, had never left Aquilo's mind for long, and he now asked the question which had been puzzling him.

'What was my father doing up here at the temple two nights ago, Vetustus?'

'Who says that he was here?'

'The Brock. He said it just before he was killed. I thought it might have been the reason why he was killed.'

Vetustus slowly nodded his head. 'You may be right. This hillside would be a good place to hide something, if that is what he wanted to do. It has the protection of Epona.'

'But why should my father want to hide anything?'

'Vincentius Clemens is a rich man, Aquilo, you know that, and travel is a dangerous affair now that the roads are full of thieves. He might want to bury his

83

wealth, hoping to come back for it when times are better. Then, when he had seen his family to safety in some walled town, he would ride back to recover his wealth. One horseman can go in secret where a great column of carriages and carts cannot.'

Aquilo's eyes sparkled with excitement.

'So somewhere there's a lot of gold and silver hidden in the ground. The staff points down to the earth beneath the feet, that's what she said.'

'Who is "she"?'

'It doesn't matter.' Aquilo rushed on, his brain racing. 'It fits, you see, Old One. That explains the Brock, and Aelian. It explains Mercury. You see, my father had a silver dinner service. It was very precious, he always said. There were stones set in the goblets, and two of the big bowls were of gold. But each and every piece of it had the figure of Mercury engraved on it. My old pewter cup was a small copy of one of the pieces. That's what Aelian was after, Old One, it must be! My Mercury cup. He thought it was one of the real silver ones.'

'You must look after your Mercury cup,' the Old One said quietly. 'Keep it safe.'

'I shall do that, of course. But far more important is the place where my father hid the real ones. I wish I knew.'

'It is better that you should not, Aquilo. Now, up with you, and off. I will come part of the way. Remember what I said, Aquilo.'

'Yes?'

'The Mercury cup,' the old man said gravely. 'It is better that you should not know.'

Chapter Eleven

It was surprising, Aquilo thought, how fast Vetustus covered the ground. Perhaps it was because he knew the countryside, or perhaps he wished to get them to the Villa Antiqua before the night was far advanced, but Aquilo found that he almost had to run to keep up with him.

Brutus showed even more signs than usual of his innate laziness. He was a dog who liked to get his head on his paws. He pulled at the rope, and tried to lie down, and whined.

Vetustus searched for a moment in the under-growth. Then with a little grunt of satisfaction, he began to pick the leaves of a plant which grew low to the ground and gave off a bitter smell when bruised. Aquilo had no idea what it was, but he watched as Vetustus rolled the leaves into a ball, bound them with a piece of twine, and waved them in front of Brutus' nose. It had an immediate effect. Vetustus gave the ball of leaves to Aquilo.

'Hold it in your hand, Aquilo, and the dog will come.'

There was no more trouble from Brutus: he stayed at heel with a discipline he had never shown before.

There was a rising joy in Aquilo's heart, the nearer they came to the villa. There was no chance of his being lost now: he knew where he was, and the direction to go. South along the green road, down the hillside, straight to his home. Felix would be there with a chariot and horses, ready to set the flints sparking with their iron shoes. A drive through the night, with the wind in their faces, westwards following the sun, and by the time dawn came they might even be within sight of the column of slaves and carts.

Vetustus stopped when they reached the ridge of the hill. The valley lay before them. Moonlight covered the fields with a pale wash, and the woods were black tipped with silver.

'I must leave you now, Aquilo. Take care. Look after the Mercury cup.'

'I will, Old One.'

'You know the way down?'

'Like my own toes, Old One. I could count every tree.'

'May Epona protect you.'

'And you, Old One.'

Aquilo looked down at the floor of the valley where he knew the villa to be. He could just make out the snake-line of the river and the square block of the mill-tower.

But the sickle of light in the sky was beginning to find it hard to cut its way through the clouds. The sky darkened, and there were no stars. Before long it was raining. They pulled their tunics about their shoulders, but the rain soaked in, quietly, persistently.

Aquilo stood at the corner of the villa yard. There was no light in the windows, no welcoming open door. He was puzzled. Felix must be somewhere, but why wasn't he there in the yard, with the chariot ready and waiting?

'You stay here,' he whispered to Magnus.

'What are you going to do?'

'Look for the horses. The stable block is over there.

You look after Brutus. You'd better have this bundle of leaves, then he'll stay with you.'

Aquilo handed over Brutus' rope and dropped the leather bag from his shoulder. It wasn't heavy, but it was good to feel his back free again. He squared his shoulders, and moved across the black cobbles to the great door at the end of the stable block.

Aquilo stood looking in. The blackness was something almost tangible, as though he would have to cut his way through it with a knife. The smell of horses hit his nostrils, a familiar smell, comforting. But no hoof stamped, no breath whispered through the still air. He could hear the rain falling in the puddles outside, could feel the cloth of his tunic sticking to his legs. The loose straw on the floor murmured to itself as his feet moved.

A creak from the door. Aquilo sprang back, panic in his mouth. It might be the wind swinging the hinges, or it might be a human hand. His knife carved the air in front of him.

'Magnus?'

No answer.

He splashed through the puddles to the corner of the yard. Magnus' eyes gleamed briefly.

'Well?'

'No horse there. Not a thing. I can't think where he's put them.'

'The other side of the villa?'

'There are some estate buildings round there, and a stable for the donkey we used to have. He might be there.'

They were walking through nettles that stung their knees and swished against Brutus' flanks. When they turned the corner, they reached a long range of low buildings at right angles to the main block. Aquilo felt for the narrow door which led to the other side.

Here was the garden where they had grown the vegetables for the kitchen. Aquilo remembered the prickly roses which his mother had looked after: they grew all along this side of the villa, climbing up the posts of the corridor and getting into the tiles.

Something must have happened to prevent Felix meeting them, something important. The message had been definite: to be at the Villa Antiqua where Felix would have the chariot ready. Well, there was nothing for it. They would just have to *walk* to Aquae Sulis.

Aquilo turned into the narrow path which led through the vegetable garden. He had expected Magnus to follow him, and he was irritated when he reached the low wall which marked the edge of the garden to realise that Magnus must still be by the villa corridor, and, more important, Brutus was with him.

'Magnus!' he called out. He jumped up to the top of the wall and sat astride, trying to distinguish Magnus' outline against the deeper shadow of the building. Something faintly grey moved towards him.

Magnus' voice came through the night. 'There's someone there. Inside.'

'How do you know?'

Magnus was silent.

'And we've got to get on,' Aquilo insisted. 'We'll probably meet Felix on the road, just as we did before.'

'There was a sound inside the villa.'

'Well, I'm going,' Aquilo announced. He jumped down to the soft earth beyond the wall and began to trudge towards the road. He looked back once, but he was not worried that Magnus still had not come. There was Brutus, too, of course. Still, he could jump that wall any time he liked. If he was allowed to.

Aquilo's pace slackened. Perhaps he'd better wait a moment. He cursed Magnus under his breath.

A shout broke the soft curtain of drizzle.

A shout of alarm, of terror.

Aquilo raced back to the wall, was over it in a moment and tumbling into the mud. Then he was up and running towards the house.

It had been Magnus' voice he had heard, and Magnus didn't shout like that unless there was good cause.

Dark figures raced along the corridor. Aquilo caught a fleeting glimpse of ragged tunics and pale faces. One big man held a sword raised in his hand.

Again that shout of terror.

'Hold on!' Aquilo yelled. 'Magnus, I'm coming!'

He vaulted over the wooden handrail and made for the fighting group at the end of the corridor. He could see Magnus now, a small figure with fists flailing the air.

The big man with the sword barred his way. The sword flashed, but Aquilo half ducked, half slipped. He was on his knees, crawling, trying to run, and the sword was frighteningly near. He slipped beneath the wooden handrail, clutching at the rose-bushes, feeling the thorns in his hands.

The sword was above his head now, and behind it a face gleamed and sweated. There was a long scar on it which ran from eye to chin. Aquilo stared, willing his legs to move and knowing that they would not. Again the sword flashed.

Chapter Twelve

From out of the black depths erupted a thing of fury, snarling, snapping, tearing. The man with the sword, attacked from behind by Brutus, turned to fend off the devil which leapt at his arm. The sword flew in a glittering arc to the ground at Aquilo's feet. He snatched it up.

The man had thrown Brutus off now, and he was struggling along the corridor, shouting orders to the rest.

Aquilo stood his ground. Suddenly Brutus was by his side, head low, teeth bared.

The man with the scar had found the steps and was advancing slowly through the mud towards him. Aquilo kept his eyes fixed on the gleaming face. He had never used a sword before, but that wasn't going to stop him now.

Then out of the corner of his eye he saw a figure at his shoulder, club raised. He twisted away, and the club whistled past his head. The sword dropped from his hand, and he scrabbled for it in the mud. He felt himself being dragged along by a force which at first he could not understand. Then with a sudden flash of realisation he knew that Brutus was running away, dragging him with him.

He was running, and there was nothing he could do about it. There was grass beneath his feet, and the thump of footsteps behind him. Noises filled his head so that he could no longer think. He knew only that he must get away from the man with the scar on his face.

He was on the western road. The shapes of clumps of trees passed him as in a dream, flints glittered in the soft earth of the fields.

Aquilo collapsed under a tree, gasping for breath. He did not know how far he had come, but for the moment he had outrun his pursuers. Brutus lay by his side. He felt the dog's tongue on his cheek.

What had happened to Magnus?

One thing was certain, and that was that he could not leave Magnus in the hands of the gang which had captured the Villa Antiqua. Who were they? Perhaps they were one of the gangs of escaped slaves which people said roamed the woods looking for food and plunder.

He must get back to Magnus. But he would have to be careful. The man with the scar on his face had not looked as though he knew what mercy was.

Slowly Aquilo got to his feet. Nothing moved in the bushes or on the road. He would keep to the side of the road, ready to melt into the shadows at the first sight or sound of danger. And he must walk, not run.

A chill breeze muttered in the branches. It came from the east and met Aquilo full in the face, pressing his wet tunic to his body. He was cold, and the further he walked the less sure of himself he became. Would it really be any use to go back to the villa? Perhaps Magnus was already dead. What good would it do anyone if he too ended up as yet another victim of the sword of the man with the scar?

But he knew that he would have to try. It was just possible that Mercury himself would protect him.

Aquilo was still some distance from the villa when

he heard iron wheels on gravel and the thunder of horses' hooves. At once he leapt for the cover of the ditch, for his head was full of the escaped slaves who had taken the villa. The noise was rushing towards him as he crawled into the bushes, pulling Brutus with him. He tried to peer through the leaves to see the chariot as it passed, but it was going so fast that it was almost gone before he could focus his eyes. He had a fleeting glimpse of a whip raised high, he could hear the crack as it came down. Stones spun from the wheels and one almost hit his face. He dodged down. There were two people on the narrow platform. The one driving had a beard which flew in the wind, but Aquilo could see no more than that. Of the other man in the chariot he had caught only an outline.

Aquilo pulled himself from the bushes. He wondered whether it was safe any longer to be on the road. If anyone else came along, he might not be so fast to get out of the way. The trees were safer. He plunged into the shadows.

His mind was busy with plans. He wished he had the sword which had dropped at his feet earlier that night, but it had felt strange to his hand, and he had no real idea what he would have done with it. Even a stick would be of some use. New wood was what he wanted, and he had his knife to cut it. It would take time, but it would be worth the effort. He felt among the undergrowth until he found something suitable, a beech sapling. He started sawing away with his knife. Brutus was quite happy to lie down by his side and watch.

Aquilo felt happier with the stout stick in his hand. It had a whippy feel to it, like a really good catapult, but there was strength in it as well, ideal for forcing a way through brambles, and for tougher work if necessary.

He did not hear the sound of breathing behind him, of leather-covered legs pushing through branches. He did not see the hand raised above his shoulder. He thought he was alone.

But something warned him, some interior sense of alarm. He spun round, but his shoulders were gripped. One of his fists pummelled the massive body of his captor, the other struggled to raise the stick.

It was tweaked from his grasp like a broken twig. His knife was in his belt, but he could not reach it. And where was Brutus?

Aquilo yelled, and his shout was answered by an enraged bark. He caught a glimpse of Brutus held in the grasp of a vast and immovable figure. He was straining at the rope, his front legs in the air, his teeth like knives in the darkness.

Suddenly Aquilo relaxed. It was partly because he was exhausted, and partly because he knew that his strength alone would be to no purpose. He dropped his hands. The grip on his shoulder loosened. He looked round.

Six of them, all standing in a circle. Big men, dressed in leather and fur, with long fair hair, and swords in their belts.

Nobody moved.

'What do you want?' Aquilo muttered.

The man behind him spoke. Strange sounds filled Aquilo's ears, but none of it made sense.

He must pretend to obey, he thought, he must do exactly as they said, so that they would be lulled into thinking that he was no danger to them.

And then one of those standing opposite him spoke, and he found he could understand.

Aquilo stared amazed.

'You speak my language?'

'I was once captured by the Romans when I was young and lived in Germany. One cannot be a slave for long and not know how to speak to one's masters.'

There was bitterness in the man's voice.

Aquilo's eyes darted round the clearing. He had no chance of running between them into the forest and escaping. They were stronger, bigger, faster.

Suddenly he thought of Felix and the games of draughts they used to play. Felix didn't like losing at draughts. He would think of all sorts of ways to prevent Aquilo winning. He would pretend he had lost a piece, or had urgent work to do on the estate. Sometimes he would jerk his knee so that the board rocked and the pieces tumbled to the ground. He called it 'playing for time'.

Again he glanced round the circle, at the thick cloaks of fur, the coarse woollen tunics, and the leather pieces bound round the men's legs with strips tied cross-wise. He looked at their blue glittering eyes and long fair hair.

Aquilo's eyes widened. An idea had come springing into his head, as though sent by winged Mercury himself.

'But that's what happened to me!' he burst out. 'My mother was captured in Germany when I was a baby. She was sold as a slave and brought here, so I am a slave, too. But my master beat me, and I ran away. I'm one of you!'

They looked at his white hair, his blue eyes, the mud on his clothes, and the scars on his arms, and he could see that he was believed.

96

'I am Hasta,' the big man opposite said simply. 'Welcome.'

'Can I have Brutus back?'

Hasta laughed, and the moonlight gleamed on white teeth. He spoke a few words which Aquilo did not understand, and then Brutus came tearing over to lick his face.

Aquilo went down on one knee, clasping the dog to him, wondering how long his luck would last. Where was this band of Saxons going? He didn't think they were the same ones whom he had met before.

Magnus. Somehow he had to get back to the Villa Antiqua. But these great fair-haired men would take him somewhere else, perhaps in completely the wrong direction. For the moment he must wait and watch.

They were busy now setting up camp, clearing undergrowth, making a fire, setting out their few simple possessions. They had food, and they offered him some. He sat at the edge of the clearing with Brutus, trying to keep his eyes open, and failing.

When he awoke, the sun was just beginning to trickle through the leaf canopy. Memory came back like a wind in winter. He shivered.

But not from cold. He could feel something furry round his neck, and he realised that someone had thrown a cloak over him as he lay.

'You have finished with it?' Hasta said softly.

'Is it yours?' Aquilo handed the fur cloak back. He stretched his hands over his head and looked at the sky. No sign of rain.

'You will stay with us now?' Hasta said.

'Yes. Where are the others?'

'They will be back soon.'

Aquilo did not hear them come, but suddenly they

97

were there. They took no notice of the white-haired boy by the fire.

'Where are you going?' Aquilo asked.

Hasta shrugged broad shoulders.

'We all take orders here.'

'Whose orders?'

Hasta indicated a man whose hair had a touch of grey about the ears. 'That is Gaeta. He leads us.'

'Yes, but where?'

'If you want food and shelter in this wild land, boy, you must learn not to make so much noise. Now, come with us.'

The Saxons moved out of the clearing with hardly a sound. Aquilo found himself part of the line, five of them in front of him, and Hasta behind. He looked round the clearing as they left. Well, he thought, Mercury had been on his side so far, so no doubt he would look after him for the rest of the day.

Mercury!

He remembered now. Last night, at the Villa Antiqua, when he and Magnus had stood at the corner of the yard wondering where Felix was, he had dropped the leather bag from his shoulder so that he could go and investigate the stables. He had not thought of it since.

He had lost the Mercury cup.

Chapter Thirteen

It was some time before Aquilo realised in which direction they were going. He tried to estimate the route by the position of the sun, but there were so many diversions that it was difficult to work out. He thought he recognised a hillside or a clump of trees, but he was never quite sure – not until they reached a group of beeches overlooking a valley.

A mist covered the lower land like a woollen blanket, the result of the overnight rain. The sun had burned it away from the higher slopes, but the tallest trees in the valley were little green islands in a white sea.

Aquilo looked at the group of alders. It was the place where they had buried the Brock. Somewhere down below the mist lay the Villa Antiqua.

The Saxons had apparently decided to call a break. They sat in a circle, eating and talking. A jug with a thin neck was passed from hand to hand, and Aquilo was included in the sharing. He looked at his dirty hands, his stained and tattered tunic. He supposed his face was just as filthy, but it hardly seemed to matter. Indeed, it added colour to his story of being a runaway slave.

An idea was beginning to grow in his mind.

Suddenly he found himself being spoken to. The eyes of all six of them looked in his direction, and for a moment he felt a stab of panic. Had they detected the lie in his story?

'My chief thinks you will perhaps know, boy.' It was Hasta speaking, and there was nothing but enquiry in his voice. Aquilo's panic subsided.

'Know what?'

'This land. Its people, its crops, its armies.'

'There are no armies left.'

'So we are discovering. Then the land is for the taking?'

Aquilo shrugged his shoulders. How much knowledge would a runaway slave really have? He kept one hand on Brutus' rough head, digging his fingers into the thick fur the way Brutus liked it. It gave him some comfort to feel the rope round the dog's neck.

'And what of the quality of the land? The crops are good?'

'Enough to live on.'

'You do not look starved, boy, so that is true. It looks a valley of peace.' Hasta spoke again in his own language to the other Saxons. Heads nodded, hands pointed to the gradually disappearing mist.

Aquilo looked down at the place which had been his home. He hesitated for a moment, then decided to take a chance.

'I know this valley,' he offered.

Hasta looked at him quickly. 'Well?'

'My master used to know the master of the villa down there. You can see the tower now. Look! The people who lived there have all gone.'

Again the Saxons spoke among themselves. The chief seemed to come to a decision. The others listened and nodded.

'When the sun is past its height,' Hasta said, 'we shall go down and see.'

They sat in the shade of the alders and watched the

mist vanish. The villa gleamed like a new-painted toy.

For some time the Saxons gazed on the alert for any sign of movement. Aquilo's nerves were tense. It was possible, of course, that the escaped slaves had moved on elsewhere, but he didn't think so. And if they were still there, so too was Magnus. If he was still alive . . .

The danger was that one of them might take it into his head to come out into the yard, but again Aquilo thought not. It was the heat of the day, and all the slaves Aquilo had ever known would have taken the opportunity to enjoy the luxury of a lie in the shade until the sun began to decline.

There was no such thought in the minds of the Saxons. At a sign from their chief they were ready. They took a roundabout route down to the valley, using the cover of clumps of trees. The buildings clearly made them uneasy: stone and brick and tile were strange things to them, and they moved across the cobbled yard with almost exaggerated caution.

Aquilo's eyes darted everywhere. Not a sign of the slaves. Not a sign of Magnus.

Silence, absolute and unnerving.

They were passing the rubbish heap by the side of the stable block. Little stealthy shuffles of leather on cobbles. Whispers as one leg rubbed against another.

An axe abruptly sprouted in the top of the rubbish heap.

Eyes opened wide, muscles tensed, hands leapt to sword-handles.

A cackle of laughter burst across the yard.

A man was standing at one of the doors, brandishing a second axe in one hand and grasping a jar in the other. He was staggering from side to side, and he was obviously drunk, but he could still shout.

Figures appeared all along the corridor. Swords and axes glittered in the bright sun.

Aquilo dropped behind the rubbish heap. Brutus barked once, but nobody paid attention to a mere dog. All eyes were fixed on the enemy.

Aquilo watched, fascinated, and appalled, as the two sides slowly advanced. The man with the scar on his face stood at the steps, his legs planted wide apart.

There was no signal, no word of command. Suddenly the yard was full of men fighting, weapons flashing, cries of pain and anger.

Aquilo slipped away, round the stable block, over the wall which surrounded the garden, to the corridor on the other side of the building.

'Magnus! Where are you?'

His ears were full of the sounds of battle from the yard. He dived under the wooden rail, and ran along the length of the corridor, calling Magnus' name. He threw open the doors. Mess and ruin everywhere.

It was in what remained of his father's estate office that he saw his leather bag. He snatched it up. It looked the same as he remembered, and he was about to open it when the door behind him crashed open and three men leapt in. He dived for the corner where a chair offered cover.

Two Saxons were circling round the man with the scar, like dogs in a strange alley. He held a sword in both hands, and its blade swung in a glistening arc round his head. One of the Saxons had an axe, the other a great club of wood with an iron head.

Aquilo crept towards the door, his gaze fixed on the three in the middle of the room. He did not see the fourth man at the door. Suddenly he was aware of leather-bound legs like tree-trunks, of a fur cloak, and a knife in an outstretched hand. He dived for the legs, beneath the thrust of the knife, and the man tumbled over his back. The knife skittered away across the floor.

Aquilo ran, leapt over the wooden rail, fell to the soft earth, ran, stumbled, ran again. On the left were the stables, with a little door in the gable end. Aquilo looked and listened.

Gingerly he pushed open the door. It was dark inside, and smelt foul. He closed the door softly and waited for a moment while his eyes became accustomed to the gloom. A little light came from a slit near the roof and picked out the black rafters.

Aquilo moved quietly across the room. He had reached the further door now. He knew that it led to the long low stables with the hayloft above, built between the eaves and the ridge tiles. The latch squealed as he moved it, and his hands froze on the wood. Nothing stirred except a little air whispering among the loose straw.

Aquilo slipped through. The stalls, with their partitions, stretched out on the right, each one of them dark and secret, a place where a man might be lurking in wait for an enemy. Above the stalls were the shadows of the hayloft.

And then with an explosion of sound and the force of a tempest, something hit him in the back. He was knocked to the floor with the thing clinging to his shoulders, gripping his head, beating his sides. He had no breath to shout, only to roll and twist and scrape in a desperate effort to rid himself of his assailant.

Suddenly he was lying in the straw with his face to the ground, and there was nobody else. A picture came into his mind of someone standing over him, sword raised high and ready to strike.

But no blow came.

'*You should have said who you were.*'

Slowly Aquilo pulled himself to hands and knees, feeling air pumping back into his lungs.

'I might have known,' he said. 'You nearly killed me.'

Magnus stood a pace or two away, his face set in the usual scowl. Then he walked to a pile of straw in the corner and calmly sat down.

Aquilo watched him in amazement.

'Where did you spring from?' was all he could think of to say.

'Up in the hayloft. When all that fighting started, nobody paid any attention to me, so I got away.'

'You nearly killed me,' Aquilo repeated.

'Well, I couldn't see who you were, not from up there. I just thought I'd get a bit of my own back, whoever it was. What's going on?'

'A whole lot of Saxons. They came with me. I thought that if I brought them here and they started fighting it out with the slaves, there might be a chance for you to get away.'

Magnus grunted. 'It's worked. So far.'

Aquilo moved quietly to the far door which led to the villa yard.

'There's four of them won't be fighting again for a bit,' he muttered, satisfaction in his voice. The yard was littered with men stretched on the ground. One man was crawling away towards the rubbish heap, clutching his shoulder.

Aquilo signalled to Magnus. He slid the great door open, just enough to let them squeeze through, and they crept along the side of the building towards the heap.

A low growl, followed by a fierce snarl, came from behind the heap, and Brutus, his rope trailing from his neck, leapt from his hiding-place at the wounded man, who fell again and lay still.

Aquilo raced in. Brutus had no time to follow up his attack. Aquilo had grabbed the rope and was pulling so hard that the dog could do nothing but come with him. All three sprinted past the heap. The road stretched ahead of them, empty, bright in the sunshine.

The woodland covered them. They crawled into a thicket and sat where the deer had made a secret clearing. The bitter smell of the animals was in their nostrils, but they were safe.

Aquilo pulled the leather bag off his shoulder and

emptied it on the ground between his feet. The bowl was there, the leather bottle, the crumbs of food, and Vetustus' snare.

But the Mercury cup was missing.

Chapter Fourteen

They were on the western road. The sun was hot on their faces, blazing from a sky of brass. Ahead of them the horizon was black with gathering clouds. The air felt close, clammy, oppressive, building up for a storm.

Aquilo had said little about the Mercury cup. He felt that he had failed, though he was not certain how or why. All he knew was that the cup was important to him, that he had risked danger, even death, for its recovery, and now he had lost it.

Magnus, as usual, said nothing, but he was company. They had not gone far, a few miles at most. The plain lay ahead of them, flat and featureless, without end. They had little energy left, but what they had was needed for pushing one foot in front of another. Muscles ached and complained. The lowering sun dazzled their eyes, so that they walked without seeing where their next step would lead them.

There should have been people in the fields, but there were none. Farmhouses on the way were barred and shuttered, or else abandoned, with tiles missing and gates torn down. Everybody had gone, either south or west, fleeing from the advancing war-bands.

Magnus suddenly broke the silence.

'Not long now,' he said.

Aquilo looked up, startled. 'What do you mean?'

'To the next town. Look! Over those trees. Smoke.'

Aquilo's first reaction was to run for the shelter of

the woods, but there was no one in sight, not even a bird in the sky. All nature seemed to be held in suspense, waiting for the coming storm. Even as Aquilo looked, the first fat soft drops fell upon his face.

They summoned the last of their reserves of energy. A bend in the road brought them to an earth rampart with a stout wooden stockade driven into the top. The gates were oak, barred with iron, and they were shut. There was a square stone guard-house by the side of them, with no door.

Aquilo looked up through the driving rain. There was a window-slit in the stonework, and he thought he could see movement behind it.

He shouted, and an answering cry cheered his spirits. A head appeared at the slit, a narrow head, long and sharp. There was a helmet on it, the plume worn and ragged. Its owner was clearly unused to wearing it, for he struggled to take it off so that he could get a better view.

'That's not a real soldier,' Magnus muttered. 'He's stolen that helmet.'

The helmet suddenly crashed into the ditch at their feet. The long thin face looked down mournfully.

'Now I shall have to open the gate,' the face said with resignation. 'You two, don't you run off with my helmet!'

As they waited they heard the clatter of iron-studded sandals on stone steps, the slamming of doors, the creaking of the great wooden lever as it was forced from its socket.

One gate opened just enough to allow the long thin face to poke through. There was a long thin body below it, dressed in various ill-fitting pieces of military equipment. Not even the boots were a pair.

'I'm on guard duty,' this strange figure announced importantly. 'Do you want to come in?'

'Yes,' said Magnus.

Aquilo climbed down into the ditch and rescued the helmet. He tried to brush the plume back into some sort of shape before offering it to its owner as a token of peace.

'That's nice of you,' the figure said. 'You can come in for that. Does that dog bite?'

'Not much,' Aquilo assured him.

The gate opened a few more inches, and they squeezed in. He was incredibly tall, this guard with the ill-fitting armour. His expression was vacant, and he looked simple.

'I am Primus Albinus Hadrianus Boscus,' the guard said proudly. 'It sounds good, doesn't it? But most people call me an ass. What did you want?'

'Shelter,' Magnus said. 'It's raining.'

'Is it?' The guard looked up in dismay. 'It'll ruin my armour.' He dashed inside the stone guard-house. They could hear him clattering up the stairs, and then his long thin face peered at them from a window above their heads.

'Go straight along the road,' he screamed. 'Fourth building on the left. Ask for Commoda.'

The head disappeared, only to emerge again a moment later. 'She's my mother.'

They waited to see if any more information would come but all they could hear was more clattering. Then the armoured figure rose from the battlements at the top like a ghost, and marched up and down, pride in every drilled movement. He seemed to have forgotten the danger of the rain.

'I hope his mother's got more sense,' Magnus grumbled.

They walked along the road. It was only a little place, two roads crossing at right angles, and no more than a hundred buildings in all. But there were people in the doorways, poor, but not starving. People working, gossiping; people prepared to defend themselves against attack, even if their sentry on guard was a sixteen year old simpleton.

The fourth building on the left was low, squat, old, and homely; no more than a long barn with its gable end to the road. Aquilo knocked. Almost at once the door opened and a small dumpy woman faced him.

'It's all gone for today,' she said. 'It'll have to be tomorrow.'

Aquilo just stared uncomprehending.

'I say it's all gone. Bread. Meat pies. Everything.'

'We were sent,' Magnus said. 'Are you Commoda?'

'By name and by nature. What's that to you?'

'We were sent,' Magnus repeated, as though that explained everything.

The woman stood with her arms folded for some time, looking them over. At length she said, 'I should have known. That ass of a son of mine, I suppose. Well, you don't look as though you'd cause trouble. You can come in. Everybody knows Mother Commoda and her meat pies. You can take that dog out to the yard. Now, who are you?'

'My name's Magnus, and he's Aquilo. We're on our way to Aquae Sulis.'

Commoda suddenly erupted into a cackle of laughter. She plumped herself down on a stool and wiped her eyes with a corner of her dress.

'Magnus!' she chortled happily. 'Well, it's good enough for a littl'un. And to Aquae? To take the waters for the aches and pains, I expect.' She laughed

110

again, a great bubble of mirth, till her shoulders shook.

'My parents will be there,' Aquilo explained.

'Well, it's nice to know you have some. Hungry?'

There was a smell of recent cooking in the low room, insistent and mouth-watering.

They sat down at the square table in the middle of the room. It was covered with jugs and jars and pots and bowls. The stone oven in the corner glowed hot.

Commoda bustled about clearing a space for them, little fat arms going like windmill sails, dumpy figure wobbling, round face gleaming. She set a pie before them. It was made in a shallow pottery dish, and the pastry crumbled brown at the edges.

'I was saving it for that ass of a son of mine, but you can have it, and welcome.'

They set to, and she watched them with eyes that looked like little black grapes in a dough pudding. The pie was hot, the meat tender, and there was nothing left when they finished.

'I can see you needed that. Now, you just sit there, young man with the white hair. That tunic of yours needs a patch. Torn all round the shoulder, it is. Now where did I put that needle?'

She was a comfortable motherly soul. Aquilo sat still while she sewed a square patch over the tear in his tunic, and tried not to squirm when the thick needle went further than she intended.

'Now, then,' she said. 'That animal of yours could do with something, I shouldn't be surprised.'

She loaded an old dish with odd pieces of meat and took it outside.

Magnus was watching the fire at the bottom of the oven.

'We could get horses here,' he said.

'Money,' Aquilo objected. 'Have you got any?'

'No.'

'Then we walk.'

'What about paying Commoda?'

Aquilo frowned. 'I never thought,' he admitted.

'Then start thinking up excuses now. She's coming back.'

Commoda bustled in. 'There's another satisfied customer,' she observed. 'My, but he wolfed that! Then he just flopped down, sighed, and went to sleep.'

'He always does that. Commoda, how much was the pie?'

'That's what I like to hear! Prompt payment. But you won't be travelling on tonight, now, will you? I can find room for you here, and you can pay me tomorrow morning.'

'We haven't got any money.'

There was a moment's silence, and then Commoda collapsed onto a stool at the table and buried her head in her fat hands. Her shoulders shook. For one appalled moment Aquilo thought she was crying, but when she lifted her round face, the little black grape eyes were sparking with laughter.

'And they call my son an ass!' she exclaimed. 'Here am I, taken in by a pair of handsome young fellows without the price of a pie between them! At least, you might be handsome under all that dirt on your faces. Off with you! The well's in the yard.'

She shoo'd them out like chickens.

'She's right, though,' Aquilo said, when he had splashed water over his face and arms. 'Filthy. Do you think we could do something for her in return?'

But Magnus had nothing to suggest.

Brutus, asleep against the wall, didn't even notice they were there.

They went back into Commoda's kitchen. 'About the payment,' Aquilo began, but Commoda interrupted.

'Don't you worry your head, young whitehair. Commoda and Commoda's ass will survive.'

Aquilo suddenly thought of the pouch at his belt. He untied it and opened it out.

One small round stone, like a coin, rolled and lay on the table.

'There's this,' he said. 'It came out of my father's signet ring. It's a precious stone, I think. Carved.'

Commoda took it in her fat little hand.

'It's Mercury,' Aquilo explained. 'My father's business sign. If you look close, you can see the wings on his sandals and his helmet, and the twisted staff he's carrying.'

'Now there's a thing!' Commoda said, laughing so that her cheeks wobbled again. 'It's the second time today I've seen that picture.'

'The second?' Aquilo looked up in surprise.

'The second time in one day, and I'd never seen it before. Isn't that strange!'

'But where did you see it?' Aquilo persisted.

'On a piece of pewter, young master whitehair. A pewter cup.'

Chapter Fifteen

Aquilo's heart leapt.

'Where?' he demanded. 'Where did you see the cup? It's my Mercury cup!'

'Now, just you sit down again, and listen.'

'But where *is* it?'

'Not far. He's a miserable little fellow, that he is. Came last night. Turned up at the gate and that ass of a son of mine let him in and sent him along here. Well, the miserable beggar sat there and ate a pie, never a word of gratitude, and wanted shelter for the night. I sent him down to the room at the end of the yard.'

'But what about the Mercury cup?'

'That was today. I took him some bread and a jar of wine, and he was sitting there looking at this pewter mug, turning it round and round in his hand as though he was trying to read a message. There wasn't any writing, though, just this picture of Mercury the way you described it.'

'Is he still there?'

'Of course he is.'

Commoda led them out into the earth yard, past the sleeping Brutus, to a little door at the end of the building. Aquilo tumbled in without waiting to be asked.

It was a bare little room, with no furniture but a stool, a table, and a low bed. The last beam of the sun fell upon the short figure of a man lying on the bed, but Aquilo could see little but a mass of black matted hair.

'Felix!' Aquilo yelled.

The man rose to his feet, came towards them with his hand outstretched, stopped as though in amazement. 'The gods are on our side! Master Aquilo, well met!'

'Be careful,' Commoda warned. 'You nearly smiled then!'

Aquilo ignored her. Suddenly all his worries were gone. Felix, the surly steward of the Villa Antiqua, was back again, and everything was safe.

'You've got my cup, the Mercury cup?' he cried.

'I have it, yes.'

'But where did you find it? Escaped slaves have captured the villa, did you know? And I left my bag there. Magnus got taken, but we managed to get away, and I found the bag, but the cup was missing.'

'There it is, Aquilo, on the table.'

There was a clutter of bowls and dishes on the table, but one piece glowed dully in the light. Aquilo snatched it up. The clay had come off and it looked beautiful.

'Where did you find it?'

'A long story takes a deal of telling, Aquilo. You remember you were supposed to meet me at the villa?'

'And you weren't there.'

'I was no match for the gang of ruffians who descended without warning. I tried to meet you on the way I thought you would take, but it's a wide stretch of country, and I missed you in the dark. I went back to the villa and looked for you, and there was still no sign, so I thought you would have taken the western road.'

'I did.'

'In that I was right. But again I missed you on the

road. I was by myself, and one pair of eyes cannot be everywhere.'

'But the cup?'

'Rolling about in the yard. The clay had cracked, and I could feel the pewter beneath, so I brought it with me. It was not until I arrived here that I realised what it was. I am glad to return it to its owner.'

Aquilo looked at the cup with shining eyes.

'And my parents? Are they at Aquae yet?'

'They are, and all are safe.'

'When do we start?'

'Tomorrow.'

Later, in Commoda's kitchen, Aquilo and Magnus sat by the oven, drawing comfort from the heat and the smell of baking. Commoda had given them a couple of thick woollen blankets, and they propped their backs against the wall with the blankets wrapped round them. They were still there when dawn came.

Aquilo blinked and stretched.

'Oh, you're awake, are you?' Commoda said, laughing contentedly. 'You looked so comfortable there, I didn't want to disturb you. Feeling better?'

'Never better in my life,' Aquilo assured her.

He waited impatiently by the well in the yard for Felix to appear.

'Probably gone to get the chariot,' Magnus suggested briefly.

They sat on the edge of the well, playing with the rope which operated the bucket, while Brutus ambled in the sun, sniffing at unfamiliar smells.

It was not long before they heard the scrunch of iron wheels on gravel and the clop of hooves. They ran into the narrow road, climbed into the chariot, and were immediately ready. Brutus clambered in more slowly:

116

he didn't like travelling in chariots, but it was better than having to walk. He would have preferred to stay with the friendly woman who laughed and had endless supplies of food.

Commoda's tall son let them through the gate, and they could see Commoda herself waving and still laughing as the gate closed behind them. The wind swept into their faces, the horses were fresh, and the sun was shining.

They had gone some way before Aquilo realised that the sun was in his eyes.

'Felix!' he shouted above the clatter. 'We're going the wrong way!'

The black matted hair of the little man blew behind him. He did not turn.

'No, Aquilo. We go eastwards.'

Aquilo accepted it, partly because Felix always knew what he was doing, and partly because you couldn't hold a conversation when the wind whipped the breath from your mouth as soon as you opened it.

Felix stopped short of the villa, and turned into a green lane which ran through trees and tall bushes. At first Aquilo thought that Felix was simply avoiding Aelian's horse-change, but the detour was a long one. He began to wonder whether Felix had lost the way. The horses were plunging now through waist-high grass and bracken. It was not until they splashed through a stream that Aquilo realised where they were. Up among trees on the ridge of the hill was the temple.

'We're going to Vetustus?' he said, but Felix only grunted. He had begun to force the horses up the hillside now, and they were no longer fresh. Where the hill levelled out into a little plateau, he pulled them to a skidding halt and jumped down. Aquilo and Magnus went to help him turn the horses loose.

Felix produced a loaf of bread and some fruit, and they sat beneath a tree and ate.

'Your father has decided that he must take his treasure with him,' he said.

'You know about the treasure?'

'He told me himself.'

'Where is it, the treasure?'

'Somewhere in these hills.'

Aquilo thought for a moment. 'Felix,' he said, 'Aelian knew about the treasure. And the poor old Brock knew. He gave me a hint, and then almost at once he was dead. Somebody didn't wish the secret known. Aelian wanted to keep it all to himself.'

Felix glanced at him briefly from beneath his fringe of thick black hair. 'That is possible. But he will not keep it all to himself. You and I will see to that, Aquilo.'

'Right,' Aquilo said. 'When do we start? We shall have to dig for it, I suppose. Vetustus would have a spade, or something useful. We could ask him.'

'There will be no need for that. The fewer people who know the better.'

'But of course you may have my spade,' a new voice said quietly. Aquilo, startled, sprang up. He had not seen or heard Vetustus, but there he was, grey hair and beard gleaming in the noonday.

Felix also had scrambled to his feet with a muttered oath. His hand had gone like a flash to the long knife at his belt, and he now held it poised.

Aquilo laughed. 'It's all right, Felix. It's only the Old One.'

Felix grumbled and muttered. But he put the knife back in his belt.

'The Old One knows all about everything,' Aquilo said. 'He told me about it himself.'

Felix looked up quickly. 'You know where it is?'

The old man smiled. 'Aquilo credits me with too much knowledge. He asked me once what his father would have been doing at the temple in the middle of the night, just before he went away. I explained the possibility of Vincentius burying his silver and gold plate for safety. It seems I was right.'

'But you don't know exactly where?' Felix demanded. His hand was still on the handle of his knife.

'No more that the deer which wander the woods.'

Felix seemed to relax.

'We must go,' he growled.

They followed Vetustus through the woodland to the clearing where the square wooden temple stood. Vetustus fetched a spade from his hut and handed it to Aquilo. It was a beautifully shaped piece of wood, as hard as stone. The blade was pointed, bound with a thin strip of iron. At the top of the blade a horse's head was carved. Aquilo remembered Epona, the goddess who appeared as a rearing horse with flame in her eyes, and the curse Vetustus had written on a sheet of lead. It didn't seem to have done much good so far. Or harm, either.

Felix was walking round the temple.

'You know where to look?' Aquilo asked.

'Vincentius' directions were not exact,' Felix muttered. He seemed even more irritable than usual, but that did not surprise Aquilo.

'The gods be with you,' Vetustus said.

Felix was now at the edge of the clearing. He had found something on the ground which interested him, a patch of earth which showed clear signs of having been disturbed recently. He plunged the spade into the soft soil. Aquilo and Magnus watched, hardly daring to breathe.

Chapter Sixteen

Aquilo had expected at first that a few moments' digging would reveal all the wealth he had seen on special occasions at the Villa Antiqua. But it was hard work, and not in the least exciting. The sweat was pouring off Felix' face and arms as he redoubled his efforts.

Aquilo and Magnus cast around looking for likely places and when they found one, Felix would dig again, only to stand back a little later and curse. Aquilo was puzzled, but he had no time to think about it. He could imagine, now that he considered it, his father giving directions so vague as to be quite useless. Perhaps he had muddled the directions, meaning south when he meant north, or fifty paces when he meant five. No doubt Vincentius himself would be able to find the place, but Vincentius wasn't there.

At length Felix sat down by the temple steps for a rest. His chest was heaving, and his face was crimson. The thick black hair was even more matted than usual, wet and shining with sweat.

'I'm trying to think if my father said anything that might help,' Aquilo suggested, sitting by Felix' side. He was embarrassed for his father. He could see from Magnus' face that he too thought Vincentius a doddering old fool.

'It was after he said that he was going across the sea to Armorica. He had something to show me, he said. You remember, Felix? You had gone to the slaves' quarters to get everything ready. I can remember hearing you shouting at the others, and then that stopped, and my father told me about the Saxons, and he gave me this leather bag, and I opened it and pulled everything out.'

Aquilo searched inside the bag and brought out the cup.

'He made me look at this cup particularly, as though it was specially important.' He turned the cup in his hand and once again traced the design of Mercury. 'The staff points down to the earth beneath our feet.' He put the cup on the ground between his sandals. 'Well, there it is. The staff *is* pointing down, but it would do that wherever you put it.' He looked hopelessly at the cup, then up at Felix. Felix' eyes were fixed steadily on the Mercury cup, as though trying to draw its secret from it.

'We could ask the Old One,' Aquilo said.

'He told us he had not seen Vincentius up here,' Magnus objected.

'But he still might know. Do you, Old One?'

The grey-haired thin figure moved past them into the sunlight. His face was expressionless.

'I do not know where your father's treasure is, Aquilo, but I do know that he left you a guide.'

'A guide? Felix?'

'Felix has no more idea of the spot than I have.' The old man's cool eyes passed over the black head of Felix and came to rest on the cup standing on the earth between Aquilo's feet. He stood upright in the clearing, tall and commanding. He used the staff in his hand not for support, but to point to the cup. Aquilo could see the horse's head carved in the wood, and he thought of Epona. Vetustus had said that Epona would protect him. He needed help now, not protection.

'The staff points down to the earth beneath the feet, Aquilo.'

Wonderingly, Aquilo picked up the cup.

'You showed me the cup before, Aquilo. Look at it now, and try to see what I saw.'

The sun was hot, and flies were buzzing round Aquilo's head. He was aware of Felix with his eyes fixed on the cup. He tried to focus his thoughts.

'The feet, Aquilo.'

'You mean the base? Well, it's all black, as though it's been in the fire. It was like that when my father gave it to me.'

Suddenly Vetustus smiled. 'And I thought we would never arrive! Go on, Aquilo.'

Aquilo's face was pink. Everybody was looking at him, and he was trying to think.

'Oh, I see what you mean!' he said excitedly. 'Nobody puts a good bit of pewter in the fire or a candle flame, or at least if they did they'd clean off the smoky black afterwards. Is that what you mean?'

Vetustus nodded. 'That is what I saw, Aquilo. I rubbed a little of the soot away with my thumb, and I saw the marks scratched in the base.'

'So you covered the whole thing in clay.'

'It seemed wise.'

'It fooled *me*, anyway. I *knew* the Mercury cup was important. So did Aelian, and that's why he tried to kill us in order to get it, but he can't have known *why* it was important.'

While he was speaking, Aquilo was rubbing the base of the cup with a fold of his tunic.

'It's coming! There!'

He held up the cup. The base gleamed and twinkled in the sunshine, and on it there appeared a circle enclosing a square and another smaller circle. Outside the larger circle were little lines all running in the same direction, except for one corner where a third circle had been drawn.

'But what does it *mean*?' he demanded despairingly.

Magnus suddenly leaned across and took the cup from Aquilo's hand. He looked at the scratch marks for a moment and then passed it back.

'The big circle is the clearing,' he said, 'and the square is the temple.'

'And that circle there is Vetustus' hut,' Aquilo broke in. 'And all those lines represent trees. And then there's this other little circle among the trees. What's that?'

'I will show you,' Vetustus said. 'Or rather, Aquilo will guide us there. It is Aquilo's cup.'

Aquilo stood up, holding the cup upside down. 'If the temple's *there*, and the hut's there,' he muttered to himself, turning round a little so that the two buildings lined up with the map in his hand, 'that means we've got to go in *that* direction. Right?'

It was difficult to keep a straight line among the trees, once the temple and the round hut had disappeared from view. There was no indication of distances on the base of the cup, and nothing to show what the third circle represented. It might be nothing more than a patch of soil recently disturbed. He might pass by on the wrong side of a thicket and never see it at all.

He plunged deeper into the wood, his eyes darting from side to side, eager for anything unusual.

And suddenly he was there.

124

A great mound of earth in a clearing, higher than a man's head and as wide as a house. Grass covered its slopes, and the westering sun cast a dark shadow.

Aquilo shrank back, and Magnus shouted because Aquilo had landed on his foot, but nobody noticed. Into Aquilo's mind flashed a memory of the valley of the tombs. Had he really seen the man with no face sitting writing at a stone table in a stone room, and his daughter, the girl with the beautiful long hair – or had it all been a dream?

Vetustus was talking, and gradually the words penetrated Aquilo's brain.

'It is a way-mark, not a tomb. Nobody lies buried here.'

'What's it for?' Magnus wanted to know.

'Many hundreds of years ago, before the good straight roads were made, people still needed to travel from place to place, to trade, to buy and sell. But the ways through the forest were hard to see, and so men built signs to mark the track. This is one such mark, the third circle on your Mercury cup, Aquilo.'

'Have we got to dig all that?' Aquilo was appalled.

Vetustus smiled. His grey beard wagged gently. 'I do not think Vincentius, your father, would have had that much energy or time. Felix, I suggest you climb to the top. It will be a vantage point from which to view the ground.' He found a fallen tree to sit on, and watched as though it was a play prepared to entertain him.

Felix grunted as he pulled himself to the top. The sides were steep, and the grass slippery, but he managed it at last, and stood on the edge of the flat platform.

'Can you see anything, Felix?' Aquilo called up.

125

Felix made no answer. He was shading his eyes from the sun to concentrate his sight on the circle of ground round the hill on which he stood.

'Nothing,' he said.

Aquilo was annoyed. 'There must be. Come on, Magnus! Give me a hand up.'

They pulled each other up the steep slope. As Aquilo neared the top, he felt himself slipping, and he grabbed a tussock of grass growing thick on the edge. It bore his weight long enough for him to get his hand over, and then one leg. He lay gasping on the top, his face in the earth.

Earth!

He looked up, saw Felix' spade resting on the ground by one of his sandals, laughed again.

'The spade points to the ground beneath the feet,' he said. 'Look *down*, Felix, not out there! A patch of earth with no grass on it!'

Feverishly Felix began to dig. The loose earth flew from the spade as the hole grew bigger. Magnus and Aquilo began to use their hands to help. Even Brutus had been curious enough to scramble to the top of the mound. He wanted to get his nose into this strange hole.

After a moment or two Felix stood back. The sweat was again dripping off his nose, and he brushed his black hair out of his eyes with the back of his hand, leaving a streak of dirt down his face.

Like the Brock, Aquilo suddenly thought. He pushed the memory to the back of his mind. He wasn't going to find out who killed the Brock. Not now. Or ever.

He watched Brutus scrabbling away at the hole. 'He thinks there are rabbits down there,' he said.

'He won't catch any like that,' Felix grunted,

126

rubbing his hands together. 'You'll need your snare for that, master Aquilo.'

'Yes.' Aquilo went on staring at Brutus' furious paws. Eventually he pulled the dog out. His nose was covered with earth, but Aquilo wasn't looking at that, but at the loose soil at the bottom of the hole. Something was shining in the brown depths. He picked it out, and laid it in the palm of his hand.

'It's a coin,' he breathed. 'It *must* be right.' He dug his fingers into the earth. He found three more little silver coins, then nothing.

He sat back on his heels. The disappointment showed in his face.

'Have you found your treasure?' Vetustus called up from the base of the mound.

'Just four silver coins,' Aquilo muttered. 'That's all.'

Vetustus' gentle voice came floating on the air, almost as if he was talking to himself.

'If I were your father, Aquilo, I think I would bury

127

my treasure and then start to refill the hole I had dug. But before I reached the top, I would throw in a few coins. It would serve to deter any stranger who might pass, notice the freshly turned earth, and begin to dig. He would think that this was all he would find, and pass on. Those who know, however, will dig deeper.'

New hope flooded into Aquilo's face. He turned to Felix. 'Go on, Felix! Dig a bit more!'

Again the earth flew. The spade struck something hard, and the sound was hollow.

In a moment the top of a wooden box lay revealed, its corners bound with bronze. Felix worked the edge of the spade under the lid, and levered it up.

A burst of light sprang from the hole as the treasure met the sun.

Chapter Seventeen

The wooden box with the bronze corners lay on top of the mound. Aquilo brushed the loose earth away, while Magnus just stared. Brutus, now convinced that there were no rabbits, had retired to the bottom of the mound where he lay down by Vetustus and dozed.

Vetustus wanted them to stay at the temple till the morning, but Felix reminded him of the distance they had to cover, and the possibility of attack. Travel would be safer by night. Aquilo agreed: he was eager to see his parents again. There was a fear in the back of his mind that they might not wait for him at Aquae Sulis. He wanted to start *now*.

They bundled the box down to the chariot, and Magnus and Aquilo went to catch the horses. It took them some time, and Aquilo's temper became shorter as the shadows grew longer. When they brought the horses back to Felix at the chariot, they found that Brutus had already climbed in and was lying by the box, guarding it.

Aquilo laughed. Then he saw Magnus' face, and stopped. Magnus had no parents to meet him at Aquae Sulis. Aquilo wanted to tell him that he would find a welcome with his family, but he didn't know how to begin.

Then they were off. A slide and a slither to start with, as the horses tried to keep their balance on the slippery hillside, then a crack of the whip, and the sound of the hooves, regular and sharp on the road.

Aquilo was happy. He looked back briefly to the line of the hills. He thought he could see the copse of alder where they had buried the Brock. Nothing had ever worried the Brock in his lifetime, and nothing would ever bother him again. He was at peace. Would he mind that his killer went unpunished? Probably not, Aquilo thought.

The wind in their faces made speech impossible. Felix was concentrating on the business of driving, and Magnus wouldn't have said anything anyway. Aquilo retreated to his own thoughts.

Words and phrases and actions arranged themselves in his mind, broke into separate pieces, were re-arranged again in different patterns.

The Mercury cup – that was the important thing. It had led them to the treasure in the earth mound. Because of it the Brock had sprouted a dagger in his chest. Because of it Magnus and Aquilo himself had been in danger of death, maybe still were. Now that he thought of it, he couldn't imagine why he wasn't already dead. Just luck, perhaps, or the protection of Mercury. The curse, however, which Vetustus had written for him to the goddess Epona, had been a waste of good lead.

They had passed the horse-change now. The last rays of the sun slanted across the roofs and made deep shadows where nothing moved.

It was something like five miles further on that Felix drew the horses off the road.

'Are we stopping?' Aquilo asked.

'For a short time. The horses can't go on for ever.'

Felix had jumped down and was busy letting the horses loose from the pole. Aquilo went to help.

'Do you think it's safe, Felix?'

The steward looked briefly at him and said, 'No one else will be after you, master Aquilo, not while I'm here. Lend me your knife, will you? One of the horses has picked up a stone.'

'There's a cottage over here,' Magnus called out.

'That's why I stopped,' Felix growled. 'It's safe.'

Aquilo went with Brutus to investigate. It was a little square stone building, one-storeyed, with a stout oak door. He tried the latch, and the door swung open. It smelled stale inside. The only light came from a hole in the rafters above a stone hearth.

'Doesn't look as if anyone lives here,' Aquilo said. 'The roof's beginning to fall in, too. Look at that rafter up there, Magnus. Hanging loose. If you swung on it, it'd come down with the rest of the roof behind it.'

'Then don't swing on it,' Magnus said.

Felix came in, holding the wooden box in his arms. He looked round, then pushed the door to, set the box against it, and sat down.

A shaft of light, thin and pale, slanted down from the hole in the roof and lit his thick black hair, his short muscular body, his earth-stained tunic and tough sandals. He still had Aquilo's knife in his hand.

'How long shall we be here?' Magnus asked.

'Time to make yourselves comfortable,' Felix said. He picked up a stone and began to improve the edge on Aquilo's knife. The movements of his hands were slow, methodical, unvarying.

Aquilo sat on his heels by the side of the cold hearth, and watched the movements of the steward's hands.

'Felix,' he said quietly. 'How did you know I had a snare for catching rabbits?'

The steward said nothing, but his hands went on working.

131

'I've been thinking,' Aquilo went on, almost to himself. 'My Mercury cup was important, wasn't it, Felix? Not just to me, but to you as well. After all, silver and gold that's buried in the ground is anybody's for the taking, if you know where to dig. You said that my father told you to come and dig it up, but you spent an awful long time looking before you found it. You had to have the map. I didn't know what I was carrying round with me, and you didn't, either. Felix, *why didn't my father give you exact instructions?*'

Felix' hands were still. His face was in deep shadow, his voice low, almost calm.

'You talk, master Aquilo, if you want to. It won't make any difference.'

'My father will want to know when we get to Aquae.'

'Your father's in Calleva, where he always meant to go. But you won't get to Calleva, master Aquilo, or to Aquae Sulis either.'

Aquilo was aware of Magnus beside him, staring at the thick figure sitting against the door in the shaft of pallid light. Everything was still. Not even the knife in Felix' hands moved.

Aquilo knew that he had to go on.

'You haven't seen my father since he left the Villa Antiqua, have you, Felix? You were told to stay behind when the column had started, and you've been chasing me ever since.

'You thought either I knew the secret or I had a clue to it. You'd have liked to have killed me before, you and Aelian together. Were you going to split the treasure between you? The trouble was that if I had the secret in my head, killing me wouldn't bring you any nearer to it. And every time you got close to killing me, somebody else was there to stop you, Commoda, or Vetustus, or even Magnus.'

The shaft of light moved slowly across the dusty air.

'I left my leather bag in the yard of the Villa Antiqua. But you know that, don't you, Felix? There were two things you told me about that night, and I didn't think anything of them until just now.

'You said you passed me on the road going west. You were looking for me, but you missed me, so you reached the town before we did. You didn't see me, but I saw you, Felix. You said you were driving by yourself, but the chariot I saw had two people in it, and the second one was a rebel slave. It wouldn't do to admit that you'd been driving with a rebel slave, so you had to lie about that.

'And then you had my Mercury cup. You said you found it rolling about in the yard, all by itself. It was the only thing you'd taken, because it was the only thing you wanted. But you *saw* my bag there, and you saw all the other things in it, but you didn't want them, so you left them behind. Well, I got my bag back, Felix, and here it is. The snare Vetustus gave me is still there. But how did you know there was a snare in the bag unless you'd seen it? You couldn't admit you'd seen the bag, or you'd have had to explain why you didn't bring it with you. After all, you said you were looking for me in order to give me the cup back, among other things. It was the snare that made me think it out, Felix. You had to tell lies, but they didn't fit together.

'Then there was that night at the horse-change when the mattresses caught fire. I thought it was Aelian, but when I saw Aelian, he was far too drunk to have done it. But *you* were there that night too, Felix. I even

133

heard you talking about the cup, except that I didn't realise. Not then.

'You had already tried to kill me, at the Villa Antiqua on the day everyone left. It was you who locked me in that room. You thought I'd be safe there, while you searched the place. I even heard you rooting about in my father's office. But when you came back, I had gone.

'I don't care much about all that, Felix. But there was something else. That fat lazy old man, the Brock. You were in the corridor when he was talking to me. You heard him say, "Ask your father what he was doing up at the temple in the middle of the night". The Brock always knew what was going on, even if he never did any work. And you knew what he was talking about. The treasure was buried somewhere near the temple. You knew that, Felix, but you had to make sure that nobody else did. So while I was away, only for a moment, looking for my father, you killed him. When I came back, the first person I saw was you. I can remember how you looked, Felix, because you were smiling.'

The shaft of light had moved now, past the still squat figure at the door, to a patch of earth where there was nothing but dry dust. Felix was no more than a black shadow. Not even the knife glinted.

But Aquilo knew it was there.

It no longer mattered very much. Not now.

His father was in Calleva, waiting. How long would he wait?

Would he at length give up waiting and sail for Armorica? Even if he did come back to look for him, this square stone prison was on the road to Aquae Sulis, not Calleva, and nobody would think to look inside a little ruined cottage off the road among the trees.

He was tired.

It gave him some satisfaction that he knew now who had killed the Brock. He supposed that Felix would finish the job now. He looked at the black figure by the door, and his eyes travelled up to the roof with its hanging beam and the shaft of light.

He'd better make the most of that light. He wouldn't see any more. So much for the protection of Mercury and for Epona's curse.

Gradually the dark shadow by the door shifted, stood, swayed towards him. He could see the knife now. It looked cold. As cold as the stone in the valley of the tombs.

And then Magnus leapt.

Not at Felix, or the knife in Felix' hand.

He leapt straight for the rafter which hung loose in the roof. His fingers scrabbled at the ancient wood, slipped, caught. The massive beam teetered for a moment, and dust floated in the shaft of light. Then with an ear-rending crash it fell, bringing stones from the wall tumbling to the ground.

Felix lay face-downwards, with the oak beam across his back. He did not move.

Chapter Eighteen

They worked quickly and silently after that. There was still a little light outside the stone cottage, though the sun had sunk below the horizon. Magnus caught the horses, and he and Aquilo brought them to the chariot. They had no trouble dealing with the harness and loading the wooden box. Brutus was already in his usual position. They left without a backward glance.

It was not long before they found a green lane heading south. They knew where they had to go – to Calleva.

Aquilo's mind was empty. He did not want to think any more about the Brock, or Felix the steward who had betrayed him, or even the Old One at the temple; and he did not dare think ahead to Calleva.

They took it in turn to hold the reins. Magnus was driving when shortly after midnight they came to a low dark group of buildings surrounded by a ditch and rampart. They wanted to skirt round it, but the noise of the wheels had been heard, and a light appeared at the gate.

Aquilo yelled: 'Drive on, Magnus. Fast!'

'We need fresh horses,' was all Magnus replied. He pulled up at the gate and waited for it to be opened.

A fat and jolly man with fuzzy hair and rings in his ears attended to them. If he was surprised to find an official chariot being driven by two boys, he said nothing about it. Aquilo was worried about payment.

'My father is Vincentius, from the Villa Antiqua,' he began.

The fat man was at once all smiles. He took them into a warm and friendly kitchen and sat them down at a table on which his wife laid food and wine.

'We know Vincentius Clemens,' the man said. 'I'm called Ursillus. And you must be Aquilo. I last saw you when you were no more than three. How you've grown!'

'I suppose I have,' Aquilo said, his mouth full.

'When was it we last saw Vincentius, my dear?' Ursillus asked his wife. She was almost as fat as he was, but she had a full plate in front of her all the same.

Aquilo's heart sank. If Vincentius had been on his way to Calleva, he must have come this way, and surely put in at the horse-change. The long procession of carts and slaves could hardly pass unnoticed.

The fat little woman waved a knife at Aquilo. 'Don't you take any notice of Ursillus,' she said. 'It was two days ago. He mentioned you would be on your way, and that he'd told his steward to bring you. Where is he, the steward, that is?'

'He couldn't come,' Magnus muttered, before Aquilo had a chance to say anything.

'Well, so long as you're here, that's all right,' Ursillus said comfortably. 'A good night's rest, an early start, and you'll be in Calleva by midday.'

Aquilo nodded. Good food was producing a glow of warmth inside him and making his head weary. Or perhaps it was the wine.

'And your father left a message for you,' Ursillus went on. 'Whatever happened, you were not to bother about Mercury, but to get to Calleva as fast as you can.

I asked him what it meant, but he said it didn't matter. Oh, and your father left money for your night's lodgings. He expected the steward to be with you, but this dark-haired talkative young man will do as well.'

Magnus merely scowled at his plate.

Aquilo sat looking at the glowing fire for a time. So his father said not to bother about Mercury, did he? Well, he *had* bothered, and it had been worth it. He'd be able to show Vincentius that he wasn't a child any more. He had the treasure in the box to prove it.

Ursillus' wife took them to a room which was clean, warm, and comfortable. Aquilo slept with his hand on the lid of the wooden box.

They were up with the sun and on their way soon after.

Aquilo tried to imagine, as the horses responded to the crack of the whip over their heads, what Calleva would look like. It would have a wall, and a ditch, and a fortified gate; and great houses inside it. There would be hundreds of people, and among them he would find his parents.

He strained his eyes through the wind-blown dust. The sun crept higher in the sky: in an hour or two it would be midday.

A smudge in the distance, grey and red. His heart rose. He was tired of the everlasting green of trees and fields, and the long dirt-coloured road. He wanted the horizontal line of grey wall with the glint of arms on the sentry-walk; he wanted the bright red of tiled roofs.

Even Magnus' face wore an expression of excitement. All their attention was concentrated on the road ahead. They did not see the rider behind.

'It can't be more than five miles now!' Aquilo yelled

138

back to Magnus, and as he did so he turned his head and saw the single horse behind them.

'Look out!' he yelled. 'It's Felix!'

The whip cracked, the horses strained. But the single horse behind drew level. They could see the thick black hair, the coarse tunic, the gleam of the knife at the belt. Neck and neck they raced.

Aquilo had no time to think of Calleva now. All his senses were fixed on the task of keeping the chariot on the road. It swayed, swerved, almost overturned, but somehow he managed to keep it under control.

He could see Felix' face, and the cold hatred in his eyes; the whip raised in his hand as he closed in towards them. Down came the whip, straight across the nose of the left-hand horse. It reared, crashed into its companion, dragged the chariot over the edge of the road. One wheel dived into the ditch, and Aquilo was tumbling over and over in the long grass, smashing into a bush. He lay still.

Sounds came to his ears as though from a long distance. A dog was barking, feet were thumping through undergrowth.

Somebody was shouting at him.

'Aquilo! Are you all right?'

Slowly he pulled himself to his knees, then to his feet, tested his legs and his arms. There was a long cut on his shoulder, but that was nothing. His head throbbed.

He looked up at the road. The chariot was lying on its side, the one wheel on top still revolving uselessly. The horses stood sweating and trembling, white foam at their mouths, but still on their feet.

Aquilo began to crawl out of the ditch. The Mercury silver was in the box in the chariot. His Mercury cup was in the leather bag by its side. He had to save it.

He could see Magnus in the ditch a few paces away. His tunic was torn all down one side, but he was standing. He had picked up a lump of wood, as if this would be enough to protect him.

Aquilo stood on the edge of the road, his hands hanging loose at his sides, his feet apart. He had no weapon, no defence. There was nothing between him and Felix except the bare empty road.

A knife glinted in Felix' hand. No word was said, no sound made. Felix' sandalled feet moved slowly, softly, across the surface of stones.

The sun was bright in Aquilo's eyes, bright on the knife in Felix' hand. Just behind Felix was the horse he had ridden, its hooves juddering on the stones, its flanks glistening with sweat. And behind the horse was the chariot.

The buzzing in Aquilo's head changed into something like the first low rumble of approaching thunder. He recognised that noise. It was the growl, deep in the throat, made by Brutus when about to attack.

A brown raging storm leapt from the chariot, straight for the man with the knife. It sprang past the riderless horse, barking and thundering, launching itself at Felix' chest. Man and dog rolled in the dust, and the knife flew upwards.

The horse, with panic in its eyes and froth at its teeth, reared. The air was full of beating hooves, shining in the sun like polished gold. Light caught the eyes which flamed and flared.

Aquilo heard himself saying, 'Epona! The curse of Epona!'

Then the hooves came down.

They buried Felix beneath a pile of stones a few paces from the roadside. They buried him with no hurry, and no words, and the horse watched, motionless. And when the last stone was laid, the horse galloped away.

There was damage to the chariot, but the wheels were still sound. The leather bag with the Mercury cup inside it lay by the side of the bronze-bound box. As the sun began to fall towards the horizon, they dragged the chariot back on the road and drove southwards to Calleva.

They could see the city in the evening light, growing bigger, stronger, safer.

When they arrived, the gates were open.